Love Have Mercy

Kordarow Moore

Love Have Mercy

Printed in the United States of America.

ISBN: 978-0-9992646-8-3

Table Of Contents

ACKNOWLEGMENTS

irst, I would like to give my thanks to the Lord for always giving me his grace and for blessing me with the ability to articulate my thoughts onto paper. To my momma love, thank you for always supporting me and loving me. I am so proud of you and how far you have come. To my Auntie Sheree you have always been a second mother to me, thank you for always supporting me, Also to you Uncle Danny. To my Brother Ace boogie thank you for believing in me and telling me that I could do this, if it wasn't for you, I wouldn't have accomplished it. To the rest of my brothers, K, Magic, Slim R.I.P and kutta, thank yall for grooming me and making me strong enough to handle anything life throws my way, I had four fathers growing up so thank yall. To My lil ladies Alarriana and Korvaya I love yall. To my little sisters Kayle and Kavara, I love you both. I would like to tell you Charneese thanks for putting in the footwork and helping us with our dreams. To my sister Shatara thank you for being here for me and helping with my child during my time away. Thank you as well Julia for having our backs, we took a big lost but we still standing! To you M.R Thank you for guiding me to the lord and giving me the understanding that I have eternal life, that is a peace like no other. To a couple of the homies, Tre Boi Perry, SP my lil cousin Moody, Brother Ron thanks for giving me loyalty and friendship. To the ones that We've lost along the way, your never forgotten and always missed, Skrew Head, Lil Darren, Darius, Bullet, Another mother to me Contessa, Uncle Meechie and the rest of the fallen Angels. Finally, to all the people that buys this book, thanks for the support and for supporting Bagz of Money, Love is Amazing so experience it with me!

Part One

*L*ove is one of the greatest emotions that we have the pleasure of feeling. Love can take you to the highest of highs or the lowest of lows. Those who have the pleasure of finding true and everlasting love are those that are blessed beyond belief.

I was once a blessed one. Having a love so pure that almost nothing could dilute it. A love that is unimaginable, unbreakable and all around perfect. But that was once... Now I'm sitting here trying to put back the pieces again. Trying to find my way through a maze of confusion, heartache, loneliness, and pain.

Wandering through this world with no destination. Wondering will I ever feel love again? That delightful touch, to again taste those succulent lips, or hold against me that soft warm body? Who's to blame for my dismay but me? Who should have remorse for my tears, or feel sorrow for my pain, now that love has made my heart stop? How did I get to this point you may wonder? Allow me to take you along with me on my journey and determine for yourself whether love should forgive? Should love forget? Or should love have mercy?

--Kyle Malone

Chapter One

"Mr. Malone, you have a Mr. Collins from the World National Bank on line one. Would you like for me to put him through?" the fairly new receptionist asked.

"No, but please inform him that we can have the conference tomorrow afternoon at 2pm since Mr. Francis will be in town," responded Kyle.

"Will do, will that be all?"

"Yes, that will be all concerning him but please hold all my calls for the remainder of the day. I'll be leaving the office soon," Kyle ended. Kyle stood from his leather swivel chair and quickly lcosened his tie. "Damn I need a vacation!" he thought as he quickly walked over to his office window that overlooked the city. He watched as the wind blew drifts of snow all over the streets. The temperature was chilly, and the clouds were grey but

his office was entirely too hot. He wiped the perspiration that was starting to ebb down his face away.

The stress lines were in clear view and told stories of the long hours he put in at the office. Mr. Malone, or Kyle as his friends called him, was the head of accounting in the

Chicago Treasury firm called Swiss Accounts. It was a relatively large corporation on the East side of Chicago.

Standing just a little over six feet with wavy hair, dark brown eyes, and skin as black as tar, Kyle projected the image of an African refugee. He started running his hands over his waves as he looked down at the cold city streets, wondering where life was taking the fast-moving traffic of people that ventured them. *Then again, who cares*, he pessimistically thought and shrugged his shoulders before turning to retrieve his peacoat from the coat rack hanging on the wall.

He lowered his head before exiting out of his office headed toward the elevator hoping not to make eye contact with any of his overzealous coworkers. His prayers were answered with a 'ding' from the elevator signaling it had arrived. Fifty-seven flights down, he got off and pulled out his iPhone to call his best friend, Lou, of over twenty years.

"Yoo!" he answered with.

"Come on man!" Kyle replied. "You're thirty-five years old and you're still answering your phone with a "yo" you got to be kidding me!" he added with a cunning smile on his face.

"Man, shut up! I knew it was you calling. What? You didn't go to work today? Or you ended early?" Lou asked.

"Nah, I had to get up outta there. I just can't understand how we spent all that money on that new ventilation system and we still can't get the temperature right. I feel like I'm sitting in the Sahara Desert. If I didn't know any better, I'd think someone was purposely tweaking the controls," Kyle replied with an annoying look on his face.

"Maybe it isn't the ventilation system that has you hot. Maybe it's the stress of landing the new accounting position that has your black ass sweating." They both laughed because Lou was right...again. So, what are you about to get into big shot?" Lou added with emphasis.

"I was trying to see if you wanted to go grab a couple of drinks and have a meeting of the minds?"

"Tell me where and I'm there."

"Meet me at Jupiter's in like forty-five minutes!" Kyle said ending the call. Jupiter's was one of Kyle's favorite spots. It was smack in the middle of downtown Chicago. It had a clear view of the lake and the food was always exquisite while dining under a soft tone of music. Jupiter's was the place to be seen, it had a mixture of rich and professional people that formed its clientele.

The after-work crowd was large as Kyle and Lou made their way to a booth. Kyle couldn't help but nodding his head to the Donell Jones L.P. "Knocks me off my feet" that was currently playing. After they were situated, the waitress made her way over to assist them.

"What can I get you gentlemen to drink today?" she asked.

"Two Cirocs on the rocks and keep them coming," replied Lou.

"You seem like the peach type, am I correct?" the waitress asked in a flirtatious manner.

"There's nothing tastier than a peach," Lou responded, licking his lips seductively.

The waitress blushed profusely before sashaying off to retrieve the order.

"Look at you," joked Kyle. "You act as if you're still in college trying to put it on everything moving."

"What are you talking about bro?" Lou asked innocently.

"You can play dumb all you want, but I want to see what you have to say when you contract something that you can't get rid of," Kyle replied shaking his head.

"So, what's on your mind?" Lou asked, officially ending the session of Kyle bashing.

"Honestly bro, I think I might've gotten in over my head with World National. This is a huge responsibility. Landing this account has put me in management in Europe, Japan, the Virgin Islands, South Korea, and not to mention China. I'll be responsible for billions of dollars. Hell, I'm barely handling Chicago, New York, and California banks and all of their mess. How am I going to be able to balance China when I don't even speak Chinese?" vented Kyle.

"First of all, you don't have to speak Chinese to balance an account. Secondly, you are one of the most talented and respected accountants in the entire world. Your reputation speaks for itself. Have you forgotten you turned down the accounting position at Berkshire Hathaway? Warren Buffet is still begging you to join his corporation. Don't forget who you are!" Lou advised.

"Yeah, I know but..."

"No buts involved in this one. If there is anyone qualified enough to handle those accounts, it's you. Hands down! Don't start doubting yourself now. You've worked hard for this opportunity. All those long hours that you put in with no fun and no sex...Whew." Lou stated wiping his forehead with the back of his hand.

"Hold on now Lou. I've been getting my fair share of sex!" Kyle shouted in defense.

"Yeah right. It's been so long you probably forgot where the hole is," Lou teased.

Kyle and Lou had been friends for a long time and knew everything about each other. They both attended the University of Illinois at the same time and graduated with honors at the top of their class. Lou was the complete opposite of Kyle, standing at a mere 6'5" with light brown skin and hazel eyes. Lou was considered to be a ladies' man. He played basketball for four years and majored in economics. He went on to establish one of the most prosperous merchandise distribution systems in the world. Making money came as second nature.

"Maybe you could get some if you'd stop thinking about her." Lou said.

Kyle answered, "Thinking about who?"

"Come on Kyle, don't play that role with me. I know you like the back of my hand. I was there with you in the sandbox scooping up sand in our Tonka trucks, remember?" Lou reminded Kyle. "So, tell me do you still think about her?"

"If you are referring to the World National Bank as in her, then yes. If not, then no!" Kyle aggressively intoned.

"Yeah, whatever!" Lou said as he caught the eye of the flirtatious waitress across the room

"Well, you can sit there and continue to play dumb. I think I got someone trying to play catch as we speak. I intend to participate in catching that peach. Excuse me!" Lou stated as he got up and headed toward the waitress.

Kyle shook his head and watched Lou as he approached the beautiful waitress. He took another shot of his drink. The alcohol was mellowing out his mood. He started coming to terms with the fact that he didn't have much to complain about. He was wealthy, healthy, handsome, and smart. He had a fabulous career and a home that sat atop a hill in an influential community. Yet, he was unhappy relationship-wise. He felt incomplete as though part of him was missing. He refused to admit the obvious and played blind to it too. The simple fact of the matter was he missed her. She was the one and only thing he did have to complain about.

Forty-five minutes later he had taken his last shot. He was ready to go home. He wished he had something soft and warm to go home with him because even though he tried to deny it, it had been quite a while since he had some.

Home was a modest mansion on the outskirts of Chicago. Six bedrooms, four baths, two mini-bars and a pool in the backyard complete with a jacuzzi. He parked his 750i BMW inside his car port and stumbled out of it wondering how he had even made it home without getting pulled over. As he slipped the house key into the keyhole, the familiar feeling of loneliness started to grapple him. He didn't want to be alone. It wasn't like he couldn't find someone or pay someone to come home with him. He just wasn't that enthusiastic about the idea since "Her."

Kyle dropped down on the couch and pulled out his iPhone to check his business e-mails once before checking his Facebook page. He scrolled through the posts but didn't comment on any of them. He wasn't one for commenting. He had a strong urge to check her page and see where life had taken her. He decided against it quickly. "How much longer am I going to do this to myself?" he thought before slipping off into a deep slumber, a much needed one...

Hold me tighter. I want to feel your heart beating against my chest. Don't ever let me go. Promise you'll never let me go...I promise you I'll protect you...I promise you I'll protect you and will never abandon you...

Those are just words to me, Kyle. I need reassurance. I need commitment. I don't want to hear it. I want to feel it. What more do I have to do to show you I love you? I'm here, aren't I? I've always been here, haven't I? But you hurt me. I gave you my heart. I gave you my all and you hurt me...

I'm sorry, give me another chance. I need you. I need you to forgive me. I'm lost without you. Please forgive me...

Beep! Beep! Beep! The alarm sounded awakening Kyle from yet another dream. "Ok, Ok, I'm up goddamnit!" he screamed at the alarm clock as he slapped it off the end table. He then kicked his feet over the side of the couch and headed toward the shower. He took off his clothes and climbed inside the shower. The cold water felt like tiny icicles sprinkling his body. He held his head under it and became fully awake. The dream he'd just had started to resurface. The dreams had become more frequent and he couldn't understand why. It had been over three years since he had lost the love of his life to a world of deceitful lies. He couldn't figure out the meaning of the dreams. Was she haunting him or was she calling for him? He stood under the water for twenty minutes before stepping out to get dressed. He had a meeting to attend.

Thirty minutes later he was headed out the door.

*****

"Good morning ladies and gentlemen!" the small, fragile old man in his late sixties announced. His hair had turned silver from experiencing much of what life had to offer and his skin looked like worn leather that had been left out in the sun too long.

"I've called this meeting today because we could possibly be on the brink of an extraordinary accomplishment. Two of our very own could be making history today by becoming the lead accountants for the largest bank in the world," the old man explained as the room erupted in applause. He continued, "After today, there will be new highs, more challenges, more opportunities and best of all, more money!"

Again, the room erupted in applause as Mr. Swiss, the old man and founder of Swiss Accounts allowed his words to sink in. Some of you in this room, in a few moments, will have the opportunity to listen in on a billion-dollar conversation. So, understand the importance of it. Kyle and Alu, are you ready to present?" Mr. Swiss inquired.

"Of course!" they replied in unison. As if on cue, the receptionist chirped "Mr. Malone, you have a Mr. Collins from the World National Bank on line one. Would you like for me to put him through?" she asked.

"Yes, Susan put him through and hold all my calls," Kyle said.

"Yes, sir," she replied. "Will do."

Twenty seconds later, history began.

"Hello Mr. Collins, how are you?" asked Kyle over the mouthpiece.

"Fairly well Mr. Malone. How about yourself?" was his reply.

"I can't complain. Just so you are aware Mr. Collins, my associate, Mr. Francis, will be in conference on this call and part of all negotiations."

"Of course, of course. I wouldn't expect anything less. Now, let's get down to business. As you are aware Mr. Malone, the World National Bank is looking to take major steps toward cornering the banking market. We are positioned in over fifteen countries. We have expressed to you our concerns of not having an accountant with determination and experience to lead us to the next level. The next level would include the Russian market as well as the Chinese market. We are looking to expand these relations and believe you to be the person of interest who could head these opportunities. Now, I must inform you, there has been a change in our initial negotiations." Mr. Collins explained.

"And what might those changes be, Mr. Collins?" Kyle asked skeptically.

"Well, we thought you would be perfect for handling our accounts receivable department, but as my team had discussed and determined, we would also like to offer you the opportunity to head our accounts payable, income, expense, and cash accounts as well."

"Wow, Mr. Collins I umm...."

"Listen Mr. Malone, I'm sorry if I blindsided you with such a request. But again, World National Bank is looking to do major advancements in the upcoming year, and we believe you would be the perfect person to help us reach new heights. Now, if this request is beyond your capabilities, we certainly understand and can accommodate you."

"Of course not! Absolutely not, Mr. Collins," Kyle said defensively.

"I am more than delighted by your request. The proposition is remarkable. We had taken it upon ourselves to become familiar with your accounts payable, income, expense, and cash departments because we figured this request would manifest. I'm sure you would understand that we would have to see the numbers before we can agree to such a request, don't you?" Kyle said.

"Well, we were thinking twenty million quarterly per account and of course food and board would be included,"

Mr. Collins stated.

"Mr. Collins," Francis interrupted, while standing tall in his grey suit. The bald spot on the top of his dark head glistened from the light and highlighted the fact that his dark hair was slowly receding. He took command easily in conversation even with his deep Arabian accent. "We're thinking more like thirty million quarterly per account, food and board included, plus a two percent annual bonus as we increase your account by a twelve percent margin," negotiated Mr. Francis.

"Thirty million quarterly, food and board included, plus a two percent annual bonus as you increase our accounts by a twelve percent margin is well received by me. I'm starting to like you already, Mr. Francis. You may now inform Mr. Swiss that Swiss Accounts just landed the World National Bank. I'm currently faxing over the paperwork as we speak. Have yourself a nice evening gentleman."

Chapter Two

Swiss Accounts was celebrating under a "Sky's-the-limit" budget following the merciless procurement that Kyle and Alu put down on the World National Bank. Champagne was being uncorked and poured without abandon by different groups scattered all over the conference room. Peoples' cars were abandoned at the office and cabs and Ubers were called to avoid DUIs.

The next morning Kyle awoke with an agonizing headache. The last thing he remembered from the previous night was uncorking a bottle of Belair Rose and pouring it all over Alu.

He rolled over and grabbed the bottle of aspirin off the bedside nightstand. He popped a few before finding the remote and turning on the news. Reporters started talking and discussing Donald Trump and the White House. Corruption, social injustice, and catastrophe were turning out to be the forefront of the discussion. "Politics, Politics, Politics that's what the world loved and probably wouldn't be crap without it," Kyle verbally complained to himself as he listened—he was almost fed up with the news. But then, something the news reporter started saying caught his attention...

"In business today, a Chicago accounting firm Swiss Accounts, landed a multibillion-dollar contract with the World National Bank. Swiss Accounts accountants Kyle Malone and Alu Francis, were named as heads of all major accounting for the exclusive corporation, which has become the largest banking entity in the world. After years of financial difficulty and diabolical scrutiny, World National Bank CEO, Samuel Collins, revived the bank and turned it into the czar it is today."

Kyle's cell phone started to ring.

"Hello?" he answered.

"Hey chilli, I just seen your name mentioned on the news. Hurry up! Turn to it!" Big Mamma screamed with excitement.

"I'm tuned in already Big Mamma,'" Kyle replied.

"Well, why don't you sound excited then? This is excellent news chilli!" Big Mamma exclaimed.

"I'm just not feeling too good today," Kyle responded.

"Well, I know just what you need to boost your spirit. Come on over here so I can fix you a plate. I cooked some friend chicken, chitlin, the cornbread is baking right now, black-eyed peas, sweet potatoes, collard greens, mashed potatoes, green beans, dressing, macaroni and cheese, and last but not least your favorite: double-layered caramel cake."

Kyle couldn't help but smile because Big Mamma knew the way to his heart...through his stomach.

"I'm on my way," he replied before ending the call. Kyle laid his head back against the pillow and stared at the ceiling. He had a lot to think about and tried gathering his thoughts before heading over to Big Mamma's. Life as he knew it had just changed. Money wouldn't make or break him, but it had the tendency to make a difference. He realized that landing the accounting position made him one step closer to where he wanted to be career-wise, but he still had some serious reflecting to do in other areas in his life as well. Approaching thirty-six, Kyle knew he wasn't getting any younger. He had dreams of one day having a wife and kids but couldn't see himself having a family if Erica, the woman that captured his heart, wasn't part of it. To him, life just wasn't the same without her. He wondered was she married? Did she have any kids? Was she happy? His thoughts suddenly switched back to Big Mamma.

Big Mamma was his heart and soul. She was his guider and advisor. Big Mamma got her name because everything about her was big. She had a big, booming voice, a big, caring soul, and an even bigger heart. Big Mamma raised Kyle from an adolescent after rescuing him from foster care. Kyle never had the opportunity to know his biological parents because he was given away at birth. Big Mamma and Poppa Malone raised him as if he was their very own.

Growing up, Kyle was loved and was taught to love others the same way as well...One thing he knew was he couldn't hide nothing from her. That fact alone is what made him avoid discussing his situation with Erica. He knew Big Mamma could see right through him, with her unique ability to recognize his pain and make him face the things he was running from; he wasn't ready to hear the truth from her. A part of him wanted to see her because he needed her wisdom and advice, now more than ever.

He reached over and snatched his phone and dialed his favorite spot to order roses from. He ordered a dozen pink and a dozen red with a few lilies to dot the bundle just the way Big Mamma liked. Then he went and took a shower. Thirty minutes later, he was on his way over to her house.

Big Mamma had the oldest house on the block, better yet, she had the oldest house in the entire South Side of Chicago.

The red brick Victorian-style home was built in 1802 and had seen better days. Originally from Alabama, Big Mamma's great, great, great grandfather had migrated to Chicago to escape oppression in the South. Bouncing from steel mill to steel mill, he saved every dime he made and invested in their home. Four generations later the home remained in the family. Over the course of a year, the neighborhood had become ridden with poverty and crime. Drugs were being sold on almost every street corner and gun shots could be heard on a daily basis.

Big Mamma could remember the times when the neighbors looked after one another and even had the right to discipline each other's children. Now, the working class had turned into the drunken class. Burglaries occurred often and no one was safe from the steady gunfire that rang out from gang rivalries. Kyle had tried time and time again to convince Big Mamma to allow him to purchase her a home in a better part of the city but was met with her stern resistance every time. He could still hear Big Mamma now... "This house has been in this family for more than a hundred years. I'm not about to let no gangbangers run me out of it. My father didn't and neither did his."

All she would permit him to do was install a security system. He prayed to the higher up to protect the stubborn old lady.

"Heyyy chilli!" Big Mamma screamed as Kyle walked inside the house clutching flowers. "Hey yourself, Big Mamma," Kyle replied as Big Mamma embraced him in a motherly hug. "Here, these are for you," he added, handing her the roses.

"Thank you, baby. You didn't have to bring me roses."

"That's the least I could do for my favorite lady," he answered.

"You probably say that to all your ladies, chilli," Big Mamma replied with a hint of jealousy

"No, just you Big Mamma. You're my number one lady," he said kissing her forehead.

"Go grab that vase off the table for me baby and fill it up with water so I can put these beautiful things in it. I don't need them dying before I get to enjoy them. Take that coat off boy. You act as though you never experienced windy city weather before," she fussed.

Kyle began to obey her orders as he started shedding his jacket.

"Big Mamma, what's that smelling good?" He asked jokingly to let her know he was ready to eat.

"That's good 'olé fashioned soul food, chilli. Go ahead and wash yo hands while I put the finishing touches on it and set the table."

Kyle was eager to do as he was told. There weren't too many things on this planet that he liked better than Big Mamma's cooking.

As soon as all the dishes were laid out on the table, Big Mamma discarded her apron. She sat down at the table and gazed at her son. She loved him like any mother would love her own kids. Kyle peered back at her with the same affection. Then he looked down at the table with all the food covering it. You would think that the meal was fit for twenty instead of two. Big Mamma made sure she put a little bit of everything on it and a little bit of everything was going on your plate if she had anything to do with it.

"Now bow your head son and lead us in grace!" Big Mamma commanded.

"Thank you, Lord, for blessing us with another day and another meal," he began. "Thank you for giving Big Mamma the strength to cook this meal and the love she put into it. Please give those who are less fortunate your future blessings and that they will be stronger in life. Help those that are lost find their way. In Jesus' name, Amen."

Kyle and Big Mamma wasted no time digging in without any words exchanged. Soon after, all you could hear was a bunch of smacking and sipping as food was devoured. By the time Big Mamma brought out the layered caramel cake, Kyle was in a food coma, but he found a miraculous way to put it down.

"Thank you, Big Mamma. I didn't think I could get another bite down. Everything is so delicious though," Kyle said as he rubbed his stomach.

"You're welcome, chilli. Why don't you put your dishes away and meet me in the living room so we can spend some time together?"

Kyle slowly did as he was instructed and made his way to the living room. The perfumed scent that permeated from the roses was strong. Big Mamma was sitting in her rocking chair slowly rocking back and forth with her eyes closed. The soft hum of an old tune was emitting from her nose. Big Mamma seemed to always be at peace no matter what the circumstances were. After Poppa Malone passed away ten years back from a heart attack, Kyle thought she would soon follow, but she endured her sorrows and worries. She was the definition of strength, and faith was her middle name.

"Don't just stand there looking at me chilli, sit down somewhere!"

"How did you know I was standing here if you got your eyes closed?" Kyle asked.

He was once again amazed by her superhuman intuition.

"Because I can feel your presence in my soul and your problems in my heart. Speaking of which, why don't you tell me what has been bothering you?" she said with a motherly tone. Kyle became quiet for what seemed like an eternity. He knew Big Mamma was a patient one and would wait until he found the words.

"Nothing is really bothering me," he lied, trying to put up a smokescreen.

"Your mouth is saying one thing, but your eyes are saying another. So imma sit right here until it all comes out your mouth," she replied.

"I don't even know where to begin!" Kyle exclaimed with a sigh.

"Just start where it's easiest chilli and the rest will come," Big Mamma intoned. She was suddenly becoming keenly alert. Again, Kyle became quiet. He had so much built up inside of him. He had so much he wanted and needed to say and knew that Big Mamma would listen. He slowly allowed the truth to come out. "I miss her!" he helplessly admitted. His shoulders were slumped like he didn't have any more hope in his body. "Sometimes I feel as if I'm losing control of myself, I'm not sure if I'm coming or going sometimes, I've never felt this way before. I've asked God to guide me, but I find myself lost at every turn. I often pray she'll eventually return one day. I find myself yearning for her more and more as each day passes. I can't stop thinking of how I messed up my blessing. How was I foolish enough not to realize what I had? What I do know is I can't move forward in life without her."

Silence filled the room when he finished. Big Mamma allowed for precious time to take its place as she watched and studied him closely. She raised that boy. She raised him to be honorable, truthful, and a man. She taught him to speak his mind and to never fear or hide from his emotions.

She was never one to impose, but she knew this time would come because she had been knowing for quite some time him and Erica had broken up. She had waited patiently for him to come to her with it.

"Baby, we all make mistakes in life, especially while trying to find our way. We never realize how much of an impact those bad experiences will have on changing us and molding us into the person we become. Sometimes we don't think those mistakes affect the ones we love, but they do. Sometimes we even end up hurting the ones we love the most. But what you must understand is forgiveness can always be found if you seek it."

"I don't think that she will ever forgive me, Big Mamma. The pain I caused could be seen in her eyes. I never seen her hurt so badly. She trusted me and I betrayed her trust," Kyle told her.

"Have you ever tried reaching out to her and letting her know how you feel?" Big Mamma asked.

"I don't think I'm prepared to hear what she has to say."

"Then you are afraid to be forgiven," Big Mamma softly said with a serious expression on her face. "How do you know she's not waiting on you? If you don't take the chance, then you'll never know. I've always taught you that if you make a mistake, be man enough to..."

"Man, enough to fix it!" Kyle finished her sentence with fierce determination.

"That's it now baby, pick yo head up before you bump into something you'll regret. Go get 'yo woman before it's too late!"

*****

After Kyle left Big Mammas, he headed over to Jupiter's. What he needed right at the moment was to listen to some good music and sip on something refreshing while he contemplated his next move. Big Mamma always gave him a lot to think about. What she said kept playing over and over in his head..."If you don't take the chance, you'll never know..."

He wondered whether she ever thought about him? Did she long for him? Ever? Or did she miss him like he missed her? What if she was waiting on him to make things right? A chance had to be taken and there was no better time than now... I still have your picture in a frame, I still hear your footsteps down the hall. I swear I hear your voice it's driving me insane. How I wish that you would call to say...

Hearing Brian McKnight's voice boom through the speakers made Kyle reminisce on the good times he once shared with Erica. He could still remember the first time he told her he loved her. He remembered that phone call they'd had like it was yesterday. The conversation flowed because they were young and very much in love...

They spent hours that night, never minding the fact they had school the next day.

He remembered the seconds that passed as they said goodnight and could feel that she wanted to say something more. His heart was beating loudly as the silence followed. Then he found those magical words and said to her..."I love you Erica." The silence continued until she responded with, "I love you too Kyle."

At the time, neither fully understood what those words meant. All they knew was that they were feeling something out of the ordinary for each other that they never felt before. They were each other's first and only love and that's all that mattered.

Kyle decided he'd finally had enough. He'd had enough of everything—the constant wonders, the dreams, and most of all, feeling sorry for himself.

He took another shot of raspberry Ciroc, pulled out his iPhone, and called the Twin City International Airport and booked a one-way, first class flight to Minneapolis, Minnesota. The time had come for him to get his woman back. The right song was playing on his way out...

Do I ever cross your mind...anytime? Do you ever wake up reaching out for me? Do I ever cross your mind...anytime? I miss you...

Chapter Three

Her luscious lips twisted into a thin line of concentration. She was feeling lucky today as she pulled down the lever to the slot machine. She was sitting inside Mystic Lake Casino in a tight-fitting red dress with her red heels on to match. Red was her lucky color.

She watched as the first column landed on three cherries. She rubbed her hands together and prayed to lady luck that the second column would do the same. Her excitement really started to show as the next column revealed another three cherries. "Come on lady luck, come on now!" she shouted as she watched the third column in a shuffling spin. When it stopped, she couldn't believe the three cherries that showed. The machine started dinging and lights started flashing as gold coins cascaded out of the machine.

"I won! I won! I won!" she screamed in excitement. Erica had finally hit the jackpot on a slot machine. A crowd started to gather as security came over and guarded her as she collected her winnings. She quickly scooped the coins into a plastic bin the casino had provided her. She really wasn't one to risk her money on gambling but found her way at Mystic Lake because of the constant nagging her friend Cante bombarded her with. The chances of the casino winning it back at the slot machine were slim to none because she was done playing. Instead, she made her way over to the craps table where she found Cante sweating profusely as she shook the dice in both hands.

"Mommy needs a new pair of shoes," Cante said loudly as if the dice were at her beck and call.

She released the dice and let them roll. She watched them land on double sixes. "Double six is a crap Ms. Lady. We have a loser," the dealer announced.

Cante was frustrated from losing a hundred dollars. She swirled the chair with a defeated look on her face. She instantly frowned upon seeing Erica standing behind her. "Now, that explains why I couldn't win," she stated. "Had I known your bad luck ass was behind me I wouldn't have never shot the dice."

"Girl, don't blame me for your misfortune. If I'm such bad luck, why did I just hit on the slot machine?"

"So that was you I heard over there screaming like a bitch in heat?" Cante teased.

"Yes, miss thang, you can just call me lady luck," Erica replied while placing one hand on her hips and snapping her fingers with the other.

"Okay, if you're so lucky miss lady luck, why don't you take a chance on the craps table. If you roll a seven or eleven on the first roll it pays triple. What'd you think about that?"

"Well, I never been one to shy away from a challenge and I've never been scared of getting some money baby," Erica said before continuing. "Hey dealer, hand me those dice. I'm trying to bet a thousand on seven and eleven."

"Okay ladies and gentlemen. We have a new better at the table and she's feeling lucky I might add. What is your name miss, if you don't mind me asking?"

"You can just call me lady luck!" Erica proclaimed.

"Okay ladies and gentlemen. Lady luck has the dice. With a name like that how could she lose? Please, place your bets. If you're not in, you cannot win. Seven or eleven pays triple on the first roll ma'am," stated the dealer.

Bets were placed as Erica began to shake the dice. She looked at Cante and winked then blew on them for good measure and let them roll. "Mommy needs a new Berkin bag," she screamed trying to imitate her friend. The first dice landed on a six. The entire table consisted of about eight on-lookers as they stared anxiously as the second dice rolled, flipped and flopped before stopping.

"Seven it is!" announced the dealer. "We have ourselves a winner!"

All the betters that surrounded the table erupted in a frenzy, especially Erica as she shouted, "yes! yes! yes! yessee! I won again!" She held the face of surprise as she collected her three thousand dollars. "Do you believe me now?" she said to Cante. "Now, let's get up out of here girl before these people start to think I'm cheating them."

******

Erica accelerated her Bentley to well over ninety miles per hour on Main Street as she left the casino. She glanced in her rearview for any police cruisers that might've gotten behind her. She was in a rush to get home and share the news of her winning with her boyfriend.

After ten minutes of careless driving, she pulled into her home and parked in the driveway. Her cell phone beeped indicating that she had a new text message. It was from Cante. "You're the luckiest girl alive..." it read.

She climbed out of her car with a squeal and started yelling her boyfriend's name before she made it all the way inside the house. "Hey Arnold, Arnold baby I won!" she shouted.

"Whoa, whoa, whoa. Honey, what's going on? What's all the yelling about?" He questioned as he entered the foyer. He had to brace himself as she jumped into his arms. "Baby, let me tell you." Erica said as she placed kisses all over his face. "First, I hit the slot machine for a jackpot, then Cante, not believing in your girl, dared me to try my luck at the craps table. You know your baby don't back down from a challenge, right? So, I put a thousand dollars on seven and eleven which paid triple on the first roll- and bang! What do I do? Hit a seven!" she finished, out of breath with excitement.

"That's wonderful baby!" Arnold replied with a look of amusement on his face. He knew Erica could get really excited at times and now was one of those times. "So how much did you win Erica?"

"No baby don't call me Erica anymore. From now on, call me lady luck," she said before continuing, "I won a little sumn sumn Mr. Nosey."

"Okay, Lady Luck, Guess what?" Arnold said as he grabbed her by the hand and led her into the dining room "Your luck don't stop at the casino."

Before Erica's eyes was a table filled with lobster, steak, salad, and a bottle of champagne. The room lights were dimmed, accentuating the ambiance that was already provided by soft candlelight. She then noticed the candles that were burning were emanating her favorite scent. She looked up at Arnold with a look of affection and surprise. It had been a long time since Arnold had surprised her by cooking for her. His job had demanded most of his time and it left Erica feeling neglected more than she cared to admit.

"So, what did I do to deserve this?" she asked playfully. "My Birthday isn't for another month."

"It doesn't have to be your birthday for you to be treated special. Because you are the queen and that's all that matters. Come here and allow me to take you upstairs and undress you my queen. Your bubble bath awaits."

Erica was speechless as she was picked up and carried away up the winding stairs. As they reached the top, she noticed the chandelier hung and sparkled in the eyes she shut to silently thank the heavens above.

Inside the bedroom Arnold began to slowly undress her.

Taking his time, he delicately removed every single piece of clothing from her body, he picked her up to carry her into the bathroom and placed her gently into the warm water. He stopped to slowly massage her. His magical hands began to relax her.

He stopped for a second to reach over and claim the flute of champagne that he had waiting for her. "Just relax baby and allow me to take care of my queen."

Arnold began to massage her more affectionately. "I love you so much," he whispered into her ear as he worked his way around her neck. "Just relax baby," he purred. "I'm going back downstairs right quick and finish preparing your meal." Erica closed her eyes and let herself get lost in the euphoria of the moment.

Arnold made it to his feet and away from Erica, instantly his thought went to the first day he seen her....

It was two years ago while attending a potluck celebration of influential African Americans in the Minneapolis area. Arnold was the Vice President of the Boys and Girls Club in the Twin Cities.

He also started several charities that focused on raising money to fund less fortunate kids' college tuitions. He was currently responsible for sending more than a hundred kids to college alone. Erica wasn't seeking any companionship at the time, being that she was still healing from the failed relationship with her ex, Kyle. She was trying to focus on herself and channel all of her energy into her job helping the less fortunate. When Arnold saw Erica for the first time that night, he knew she was just his type.

While standing just over 5'7" with long, silky black hair down to the middle of her back, she had brown skin and eyes that glowed the color of milk chocolate. By all accounts, she was breathtakingly beautiful. She was the type to steal your heart at first sight. And she had stolen Arnold heart just like that.

Downstairs, as he was finishing setting up the table, he caught the sounds of footsteps softly approaching him. He looked up to find Erica standing in a red see through negligee with a tail that was dragging on the floor behind her. She continued to approach him as her black red bottoms clicked against the marble floor. Erica was the epitome of sexy.

Arnold stopped what he was doing to prepare himself to embrace her in a loving hug. She fell into his arms. He could smell the fragrance of the Beyoncé perfume she liked to wear to arouse him. He then released his hold on her and pulled out a chair so she could sit down. He had another flute decorating the table and popped the cork on the bottle of rose and poured her yet another drink before sitting down directly across from her.

"You are so beautiful" he stated as he watched her add some of the shrimp to her plate.

"Thank you baby and you are not so bad yourself, Mr.," she retorted before continuing. "So, you never told me what I've done to deserve such special treatment."

"I realized that I've been neglecting you a lot lately. I haven't been meaning to. It's mainly due to work and all but I just wanted to take this time and show you how much I appreciate having a loving woman like you by my side. Ever since you came into my life you haven't brought me anything but happiness. I've experienced a peace like never before. You deserve this every day and if I can't give this to you every day, I promise to give it to you as much as possible..."

"That's a very nice thing for you to say, but I've always been one for action. Come and show me how much you appreciate me," Erica said seductively.

"I thought we would eat first."

"Oh, I've got plenty for you to eat," she replied as she opened her legs a little.

Arnold then stood up and walked over to where she was sitting. He bent over top of her and planted a deep passionate kiss on her soft moist lips as he reached down to touch her wetness. She was dripping like a leaking faucet. He stuck his two middle fingers inside her. She moaned deeply..."Ohhhh."

"Arn00000llllddd!" He then stood up in front of her so she could see that he was erect. Erica reached out to grasp a hold of it, but he slapped her hand away.

"This is not about me," he said.

He then slid a large portion of the food out of the way that was on the table. He bent over and picked her up from the buttocks and sat her down in the clearing. They looked at each other in the eyes lustfully. Arnold then bent down on both knees and buried his face between her legs. Erica wrapped her legs around his head and let him devour her as if she was one of the entrees....

Chapter Four

The next morning, Erica awoke to the aroma of breakfast caressing her nostrils. She turned over to glimpse at the alarm clock that sat on the bedside table. It read ten thirty a.m. "Damn!" she mumbled as she realized she was going to be late to work. It had been a long time since she slept pass six. She'd had a long night though, that was for sure. After Arnold ate her out like a monster, he carried her up to the bedroom and massaged her entire body down with scented oil before making love to her over and over again. Her body felt numb now. She took a deep breath then exhaled slowly. She loved her man very much. She lost count of how many times she had thanked God for placing him in her life. He was more than just her significant other, he was her heart throb as well. He maintained a strict regimen at the gym and was very fit as a result. He stood 6'1" with a shiny, bald head. His skin was a dark chocolate complexion. He reminded Erica of a handsome African god. Up until now, she had come to the conclusion that life had dealt her a bad hand. She thought back on her previous relationship with Kyle.

She felt the muscles in her face tense up and she began to frown as she thought back on the day her life got turned upside down...she had just completed a seminar in downtown New York. She was ready to celebrate with a nice meal because she had finished it a day earlier than expected. The event had been long and exhausting, and she was more than ready to make it back to the windy city.

That day she booked a flight to O'Hare Airport in Chicago. She'd had plans of surprising Kyle with an early return. She landed and retrieved her car from the parking ride lot. She raced down the Dan Ryan freeway at over a hundred miles an hour. She exited the ramp into Calumet City and five minutes later, she pulled into the driveway of their home right behind Kyle's Ranger Rover sport.

She hopped out and popped the trunk to reclaim the bags filled with souvenirs she had bought for him. When she entered their house, she was met by silence. She carefully stepped out of her heels and set the bags by the side door. She began to tip toe her way up the stairs as she slowly discarded her clothing. She stopped momentarily. She thought she heard a sound coming from their bedroom. She determined it was Kyle and proceeded the rest of the way and hoped that her surprise wouldn't be spoiled. She was down to just her thong as she reached for the doorknob, turned it and slowly began pushing it open...

Erica! Erica! Erica! Hey baby! Arnold repeating trying to gain her attention.

She snapped back to reality upon hearing his voice.

"Baby, are you okay?" Arnold asked as he stood in the doorway with a tray with her favorite breakfast: waffles, steak, eggs, and orange juice. "You look as if you were in another universe," he told her this with a concerned look on his face. "I'm sorry baby. I was just thinking about how amazing you were last night. You put it down so good on your girl that I had to think some more about it," she said.

"That was nothing," Arnold chimed. "What you need to do is see how I put it down on that food. I figured you'd be hungry considering the fact that you didn't have time to eat last night."

"Thank you so much baby," she said, reaching for the tray as Arnold placed it before her. "Aren't you going to join me?" she asked questioningly. "You didn't get a chance to eat either."

"You must've forgot you gave me plenty to eat."

"You're so nasty," Erica said before they both broke into laughter.

She began digging into her meal as he sat and watched her. He admired every feature on her face. He loved the way her eyebrows arched upwards when she was deep in thought. He loved the way her bottom lip was just a touch bigger than the top and the way it felt in his mouth when he kissed her. He loved her sense of humor and especially how she could be so silly and goofy at times. But what really turned him on about her was her drive and ambition.

He remembered how hard it was to get her attention at first. How she denied his advances time and time again. All it did was make him pursue her even harder; it made him want her even more. He reminisced on how many hours he spent just listening to her vent as she went through the emotional rollercoaster of wanting him one minute and valuing his friendship the next. But he was patient with her, gentle with her, and he took the time to understand the pain she had just endured...

"Oh my god!" Erica exclaimed, interrupting his thoughts. "Debra is going to kill me. I forgot to call in this morning and tell them I might not make it. We were also supposed to go over the blueprints for the new "forever united" commercial today. I am never going to hear the end of this," Erica interjected while wiping the side of her mouth with a napkin.

"Calm down baby. Remember what I told you. The number one rule is to never panic. While you was up there daydreaming of yours truly, I took the initiative and called in for you. Debra said she would hold it down for you if you didn't end up making it, so relax," Arnold said soothingly.

"Where have you been all my life?" Erica asked with a surprised look on her face. "I don't know what I'd do without you," she added.

"You'd probably lose your pretty little mind. Now, come on let's take a shower together and afterwards, I want you to go somewhere with me."

Arnold and Erica arrived at Crystal Lake Cemetery shortly afterwards. He got out of the car and made his way around the other side to open the door for her. He grabbed her by the hand and led her over to the weathered tombstone. Erica read the heading on it, "Arnold Lamount Simmons Sr."

Arnold then pulled her in front of him and embraced her tightly around the waist. The heat from their bodies protected them from the chilly afternoon. "Allow me to tell you a story that I've never told anyone before." He began, "It's a story of the greatest man I've ever known, a man of influence. My father was a disciplined man and very strict and powerful in business. He went to work early every single morning and brought his work home with him and would work late into the night. He put business before everything...besides me. He used to tell me that I was his only solace in a world filled with madness. I would get up early with him to see him off to work and wouldn't go to sleep until I heard his keys unlocking the door. He would tell me stories about taking over business. He was relentless with his business ventures. He always reminded me that business was never personal. My father was very meticulous and was never late for an affair."

"One morning, I woke up late...later than I normally would. I made my way to his study, but I stopped when I overheard him speaking angrily into his phone. I couldn't make out exactly what was being said but I knew it didn't sound too good. Next thing I knew my father slammed down the receiver. I then tapped on the door and peeked my head into the study. He looked up and told me to come in. He told me how the world was full of business politics and it was an inherently vicious world to be involved in. He told me how he had to make crucial decisions sometimes and some of those decisions end up costing him more than just money. Afterwards, he left me in the study and left the house entirely."

"I waited up for him all night, but he never returned. My father was found shot dead the next morning inside of his car. He had gotten involved with the wrong people and in the midst of a bidding war in the acquisition of a major pharmaceutical company he took a gamble that cost him his life. They took my father away from me," Arnold ended, sadly.

His voice trailed off and started to crack as tears fell from his eyes. Erica turned around and hugged him tightly. "Sometimes I still wake up in the middle of the night and find myself waiting for him. I listen for his keys to unlock the door, but it never comes...he never comes."

He broke down to his knees and started weeping uncontrollably. It was impossible for him to hold back and Erica was right there to comfort him as he let his emotions show. He had always been strong for her and now it was her turn to be strong for him.

Chapter Five

The wind's chill bit through the coat of anyone brave enough to walk through downtown Minneapolis. The wind chill factor made it feel as if the temperature was forty below zero. It had been snowing every day for the past week and the snow drifts had caused the snow to pile up on the side of the roads, resembling miniscule mountains on the roadside. The streets were slick with black ice as cars cautiously took the gamble of traveling on them.

Minneapolis was the largest metro area in Minnesota. The streets were always busy. Everyone was in such a big rush because of a severe snowstorm that had hit the city. Sitting right there in the middle of Nickelit Avenue was a twenty-story brown, brick building with icicles dangling from the roof. Inside of the building, on the third floor was a newly designed office. It was painted in bright colors with the purpose of keeping a psychologically jolly ambiance. It was spacious without the benefits of cubicles. It was an open area decorated with reclining chairs, oversized bean bags, mini fridges filled with food, and photos of all the employees hanging on the walls. It was apparent to the outside observer that the owner wanted an atmosphere with the feeling of home rather than work.

When you entered the building, you couldn't help but notice the huge sign hanging above the doorway advertising Erica's nonprofit organization's name: "Forever United Charities." Erica was standing at the head of the conference table inside the building's conference room with her MacBook Pro in hand. The pictures that were being displayed on the screen were the same pictures that were being displayed on the projection screen hanging on the wall. Her employees were lounging around in every seat available as she talked.

"The purpose of this commercial is to get younger contributors to donate funds to Forever United. As of right now, we're currently pulling in around fifteen thousand dollars a month in donations through our televised advertisements. Initially, we had hoped for at least twenty thousand monthly in the form of advertising. We have gathered through our census that our commercials are attracting older contributors instead. In order to get the extra five to seven thousand needed monthly, we have to appeal to the younger generation. So today, we are going to try out a new approach. The overall theme of this commercial is going to be help the next generation. We're striving to raise the awareness of the college students and the younger working class to the fact that their generation once needed help like the generation before them. So, now I'll step aside and allow Debra to take the floor."

Erica went and found herself a seat as Debra got up and took the stage. She was a small woman in her early twenties. You'd think she never seen a day in the sun as her skin was as pale as the snow that covered the ground. She was a rather attractive young woman that had blonde hair that stopped around the shoulders. She also had

some of the cutest pouty lips that usually got her whatever she desired. She had been with Erica since the beginning of the foundation. Debra slid her hand over her tablet to make it go to the page that she wanted to display on the projection screen. Every employee in the building was given their own tablet. It was one of the many perks of working there.

"So, as you can see here," Debra began, "#help the generation will begin with a young child receiving a blanket from the young lady in her twenties. Now, you can see here that the young child has grown into a young adult and has handed out food at the soup kitchen to a different young child. As you follow the scene you can see that the child is now an adult handing out toys to different children at a Christmas event. So, the trend is repeated. Toward the end of the commercial all three generations will be seen holding hands as they reply in unison 'Help the next generation.' The commercial then fades out and in large letters the hashtag "HelptheNextGeneration" is shown and the commercial ends."

The room was silent as the employees nodded their heads in approval. Debra began to speak again, "Okay, what you just witnessed is a rough draft. I'm looking for any ideas or suggestions on how it can be improved. The floor is open."

Everyone started glancing around the room and at their feet until someone finally spoke, "I believe the commercial is put together rather nicely. The message is concise and speaks to the younger generation."

Whispers of agreement could be heard before Erica stood up and made her way over to Debra's side. Erica put her arm around her shoulder and said, "So, if no one has anything to add then it can be assumed that we have achieved our goal here. Nice, job Deb," she said, turning to her and shaking her hand.

She again addressed the room, "We will now let Josh, our event coordinator, speak. Before you begin, Josh, I would like for you to..." Erica's words were cut short as someone entered the office and abruptly began to speak.

"Excuse me. I'm not sure if I have the right to the floor, but I'm looking for a Ms. Caldwell," the man said.

"I'm Erica Caldwell. How may I help you?"

"We have a special delivery for you. Now that it's confirmed I'm in the right place and speaking to the right person, I'll have my team begin bringing them up." The delivery man said before exiting the office. Soon afterwards several men started setting down giant bouquets of flowers. There were countless arrangements, there had to be over fifty different floral decorations brought in. Erica was in awe as the delivery men moved about. The first delivery man then came over to her and asked for her signature on the clip board he was holding in his hand. After getting her signature, they hurriedly left the meeting. "Oh my god!" Debra jealously exclaimed, this is the most romantic thing I have ever seen, Erica."

Erica looked around at the arrangements scattered all over the office in amazement. Everyone in the office was chattering about what was going on. Some of the women had their mouths agape and looked on in envy as they secretly wished the flowers had arrived for them.

Erica excused herself as she stepped into the hallway so she could place a call to Arnold.

"Hey baby!" she screamed as soon as he answered. "I love you so much baby. I can't believe you. This has got to be your best surprise ever. I love you so much baby. Thank you, thank you, thank you!" she added.

"Slow down just a little bit sweetheart. I'm a little confused. What are you talking about...last night?"

"No! I'm talking about all the flowers you sent me at the office just now."

"But I didn't send you any flowers," Arnold replied suspiciously.

"Oh, um, are you sure?"

"I'm more than positive baby. I'm absolutely sure I didn't."

Erica paused for a few seconds before replying. "Well, I'm sure it had to be one of the recipients of one of our charity events then."

"More than likely. Either way, it seemed to have really excited you which is always a plus. Not to cut you off, though baby, but I have to end this. I'm in the middle of a really important meeting. I'll call you as soon as I finish up honey, I love you, Okay?" Arnold ended.

"Love you too, baby," Erica replied then ended the call by placing her phone in her pocket.

She leaned back against the wall and tried gathering her thoughts. Confusion consumed her as she tried to think of which recipient could've sent those flowers. "How strange," she said to herself.

"What's so strange?" Debra asked as she walked up. She stood directly in front of Erica.

"Well, I just spoke to Arnold and he was totally oblivious to what I was talking about. He said that he never sent any flowers," Erica finished with a baffled look on her face.

"You know what, maybe it was the eastern school district that we did that coat drive for, thanking us," Debra said, trying to give more clarity to the matter.

"Yeah, well, if it is, this is a really big thank you," Erica said as she made her way back inside the office. Debra was right on her heels. Once inside, Erica began to look through some of the arrangements hoping to find a note or something identifying the sender, but her search ended with no luck. She then informed everyone that it was time to get back to work. Josh took over the floor again and started to speak. Erica sat in a chair close to him trying to stay focused, but her mind kept drifting to the flowers. It was out of the ordinary for either a donor or a recipient to send such an extravagant gift. Some of the arrangements looked rather expensive. She estimated the entire shipment must've cost upward of five thousand dollars.

"That's a heck of a thank you!" she thought to herself. Erica wanted to kick herself after she realized she could have asked the delivery man who had the flowers delivered. At that moment, she got up and made her way back into the hallway so she could place a call to the delivery service.

"Hello, Floral Wonders, how may I help you?" the receptionist asked.

"My name is Erica Caldwell. You just had a bunch of flowers delivered to me. I was trying to figure out who had purchased them so I could personally thank them."

"Okay," the receptionist said. You said your name is Erica Caldwell, correct?" "Can you give me the address where the delivery was made?"

"Yes, it was 2037 Nickelit Avenue on the third floor."

"Okay, okay, let me see here," the receptionist replied as she began typing in the information. "Well, all I have here is that the sender wanted to remain anonymous."

"Anonymous!" Erica repeated, "Is that a normal request?" she asked, annoyed.

"Well, we have had customers request that in the past, but I wouldn't say it's that common." "It says right here in a side bar that the sender gave strict orders that they didn't want to be identified."

"Is it possible for you to tell me the cost of the arrangements?"

"Yes, I can do that. Let's see..." the receptionist could be heard pecking on the keyboard in the background.

"Wow, the total came to seven thousand three hundred and fifty-five dollars and ninety-seven cents. Someone must really love you!" she added.

"Um...thank you for your assistance and have a very nice day." Erica ended the call and walked back over to where Debra was and got her attention by waving her over. When she was within speaking distance, she said, "I'm sorry, I have an emergency to attend to. Please excuse me. Before the day ends, I have something I want you to do. First, I want you to go through the flowers to see if a note or something was left. Second, I want you to let everyone here today pick whatever they want out of the arrangement for themselves. Finally, once Josh has gone over the events and Karen has discussed the budgets, I want you to order personal pan pizzas for everyone. I want everyone to relax and enjoy the rest of the day."

"Consider it done," Debra replied.

Erica left the building, then immediately called Cante, "Hey Ms. Lady Luck. What'cha doing?" Cante answered.

"Okay enough with the Lady Luck. This is really serious. I have an emergency."

"What's going on?" Cante asked with sudden concern showing on her face.

"I need you to meet me at Chipotle in Crystal Lake. I'll tell you everything once we are there."

"Give me twenty minutes. Max. Can you please order me a burrito bowl? I haven't eaten anything all day."

"I'm having a crisis and all you can think about is a burrito bowl? Bye, girl," ended Erica.

*****

Ten minutes later, Erica pulled into Chipotle. She entered and ordered two burrito bowls and took a seat at the back booth. Five minutes later, Cante entered and made her way over to Erica.

Cante looked amazing as usual. A mixture of native and African American with the skin tone of gold and shoulder-length silky, black hair. Her eyes were a mesmerizing earth-tone green and she stood much taller than the average female at six feet tall.

"Hey," greeted Cante as she sat down and grabbed hold of one of the burrito bowls. "What's going on that's so drastic that I had to rush here?"

"Okay, do you remember when I first made it to Minnesota and did that joint charity event with the guy Earl? He was on the-board of directors for the school district," Erica asked.

"Of course, you talking about Earl that kept coming on to you and didn't understand the word 'no'?"

"Exactly, well, girl, I believe he is back," said Erica while looking over her shoulder.

"What makes you say that?" Cante asked with a paranoid look. "Because today while at work a delivery guy entered and said that he had a special delivery for me. In comes about five more delivery men carrying with them fifty floral arrangements. I called Arnold to thank him for the surprise and he was just as shocked as I was. He claims that he never sent any flowers."

"It could've been someone you did charity work for giving you a thank you."

"Initially, that thought had crossed my mind, so I began by trying to track the arrangements through the company that sent them but Floral Wonders, the company, told me that the sender gave instructions that they wanted to remain anonymous."

"Anonymous..." repeated Cante.

"Strange, right?" So, then I asked them what the total cost of the purchase was and guess what they told me?"

"What?" she asked.

"Seven thousand three hundred dollars and some change," Erica said bluntly.

"Oh my...yeah, that would be a mighty expensive thank you. Especially from someone that needs charitable donations and the like."

"Exactly, see girl, imma bout to call the police and get a restraining order put on this guy from the school district. I do not have time for this kind of thing again," Erica said.

"Hold on, slow down just a little bit. First off, you don't even know if he's the culprit. Secondly, you can't just go placing restraining orders on people based on suspicion. Remember, I told you that his sister and I share the same hairdresser I'll just call her to see what he's been up to. But if I remember right, he moved to Florida and is getting married soon. Just give me until tomorrow to clarify before you go reporting people," stated Cante.

"Okay, but if something happens to me before then, you know who is responsible." Cante broke into laughter before she spoke. "You are seriously something else. You need to relax and sooth your mind. How about we go to Club Seven tonight, eat some good food, and listen to some good ole music. You can drag Arnold along and have him bring that sexy friend of his, Steve," said Cante.

"You're right. Tonight, is supposed to be date night for Arnold and me anyways. I don't see why Club Seven can't be the destination. I'm pretty sure Steve will accompany him, I heard he has a little thing for you," replied Erica.

"For real, girl, spill the beans!" replied Cante excitedly. Erica began to laugh before she spoke, "There aren't any beans to be spilled. Arnold just mentioned to me that Steve said that you are very appealing to the eyes and that he asked if you had someone special in your life." I hope that you told him that I'm happily single and when were you planning on telling me this?" questioned Cante angrily. Again, Erica laughed before she spoke, "I'm telling you now, you know I don't like to play match-maker for nobody. Besides, when are you going to find you a nice man to settle down with?" questioned Erica.

"When they stop making different types of men. You see, sometime I might be in the mood for a dark handsome man, or I might just wake up one day with an appetite for a white military man and then of course there are Asian men, tall men, muscular men and skinny men...Uhm,

Uhm, Uhm, there are just too many men for me to be focusing on one," joked Cante.

Erica and Cante both broke out into laughter. "You are just too much for one person to deal with," said Erica while shaking her head.

"Exactly, now you understand me. But on a more serious note, we are on for tonight still, right? Because I feel like dancing."

"Yes, we're on. I'm gone meet Arnold at home within the hour. I'll let him know that you are requesting Steve's presence and we'll meet you at Club. Seven around ten o'clock tonight." With that, Erica and Cante both got up, gave their customary hug and kiss, and then went their separate ways.

Chapter Six

Club Seven was full of life even on a cold winter night. The line to get in was wrapped around the side of the building with anxious men and women ready to go party. Arnold and Erica pulled up and allowed the valet to park their car. They didn't have to wait in line because, unbeknownst to Erica, Arnold had reserved the V.I.P. section on the rooftop weeks in advance. The bouncer lifted the red velvet rope and then allowed them inside. They walked alongside the bar before heading up the stairs to the rooftop.

When they entered the balcony, they were caught off guard by a crowd that screamed "SURPRISE!"

Awaiting them were Erica and Arnold's friends from Chicago, Arnold's closest friends, along with Cante and Steve. Erica looked over at Arnold with a questioning look in her. eyes. She couldn't believe everyone was there. Arnold grabbed her by the hand before standing directly in front of her. Slowly, he went down to one knee and pulled out a box that contained at five karat, diamond wedding ring.

"Erica, from the day I first laid eyes on you, I knew you were someone special. I also knew that I wanted you to play a part in my life. I've never been as happy, satisfied, and fulfilled as I have been with you, Erica Caldwell. There is no future in me if you aren't a part of it. You complete me and from this day forward I would like to be the man that completes you. So, Erica Caldwell, will you make me the happiest man alive and marry me?"

Erica looked down at Arnold and tears began to fall from her eyes. This had been the man that picked her up when this world had knocked her down. When she had lost faith within herself and didn't have much to believe in, he had given her hope. He was always patient with her, loved her carefully and consistently. He had protected her from her fears, accompanied her in her loneliness and wiped away her tears at her weakest. There were times in which she questioned if he was the right man for her, but here, at this moment looking down at him, there wasn't a doubt in her mind that he was the man for her. Out of the crowd of family and friends she heard someone yell, "Say yes girl!" A slight chuckle came from inside of her as she wiped away a tear.

"Yes! Of course, I will marry you, Arnold."

Erica held out her hand as he put the ring on her finger. He rose up and scooped her up, holding her close to his body as they spun around in circles. Everyone in attendance began to clap and cheer as Musiq Soul Child's voice filled the room. (I'll love you when your hair turns grey (yeah) I'll still want you if you gain a little weight (yeah) the way I feel for you will always be the same, just as long as your love don't change ...lately you've been questioning if I still see you the same way, cause through these trying years, we've all and all physically changed, girl don't you know you'll always be the most beautiful woman I know and even when you get on my last nerves, I couldn't see myself being with another girl...)

Erica sat at a table with her father, mother, and Arnold while everyone around them danced.

"So, Arnold," Mr. Caldwell began. "What are you planning with my beautiful princess now that you have her for the rest of your life?" he questioned.

"Well, we haven't really discussed it, but, I'm sure some children will be part of our conversation."

"Arnold!" said Erica as she playfully slapped him on the arm, slightly embarrassed.

"Actually, you'd make me a very happy man if you two were to give me some grandchildren," confirmed Mr. Caldwell.

Erica looked at her father astonished. He had always been a difficult man to please, he didn't believe there was a man on earth deserving of his baby girl. He was very overprotective of her being that she was their only child. When things went south in Chicago, she had moved to Minnesota to be closer to him and her mother. She had cried on his shoulder with her broken heart and he gave her the love and guidance that only a father knew how. He had witnessed her transformation from then until now and knew that Arnold played a major part in her happiness. So, when he came asking for her hand in marriage, he had happily given his blessing.

"Hopefully I can make you a really happy man, really soon," said Arnold, leaning over and giving Erica a kiss on the cheek.

"Excuse me Mr. and Mrs. Caldwell, Arnold, may I please steal the lady of the night for a second?" interrupted Cante with Steve by her side. She grabbed Erica by the hand and pulled her to the side.

"I believe Steve and I are about to make our great escape, congratulations again girl, please let me see that beautiful ring one more time," Cante said.

Erica put out her hand and allowed the facets to glisten before Cante eyes.

"He is such a lucky man," said Cante before continuing, "oh, and before I forget, those flowers didn't come from Earl. Sorry to hurt your feelings but he's happily married, and they are expecting."

Erica made her way over to sit by Arnold's side. She tried listening in on the conversation that he was having with her father but was sort of distracted by the news she had just received from Cante. Tonight wasn't the time to go trying to figure out the mystery of the flowers but she would make it a point to get to the bottom of it. She looked around as the roof top began to clear out as the guests slowly exited.

"May I have this last dance?" whispered Arnold in her ear.

"Of course."

They got up and made their way onto the dance floor followed by Mr. and Mrs. Caldwell. The foursome began to slowly dance to Eric Benet and Tamia's "Spend My Life."

*****

The next morning Erica awoke from her sleep, feeling Arnold's strong arms holding her against his chest.

"Good morning sweetheart, you must have been sleeping really good...you were talking in your sleep."

"Oh my! Yes, I was so exhausted. I must have been dreaming about a million things," she replied while trying to figure out exactly what she had dreamed of. "Cante called several times, she was wondering whether you were still going to meet her at the mall."

"Of course, I almost forgot. What time is it exactly?"

"It's twelve noon."

"Huhh," Erica sighed before nestling back into Arnold's chest. Breathing in his scent, feeling the muscles in his chest contract, she began to feel like she could lay there forever.

A smile spread across her face because she felt an overwhelming sense of happiness. Finally, she felt that she had found her king. She kissed him about his chest before whispering that she loved him.

"I love you too, Erica."

"Huhh, baby, I don't feel like getting up but if I don't, I'd never hear the end of it from Cante."

"It's okay, I have a few errands to run anyways. Besides, I know better than to get in the way of a woman and her psychotic addiction to shopping," he joked.

"Shut up, you don't hear me saying anything about men and their psychotic addiction to those big, nasty weights," quipped Erica.

"That's because women love the results we get from those big, nasty weights! While on the other hand, we men dread the day the credit card statements come in the mail after one of your shopping sprees...and they say that love don't cost a thing."

Erica began to laugh because she knew that what he was saying was true. It was times like these when she felt the most content, laughing and joking with her man that she was in love with without a care in the world.

Finally, she muscled up enough strength to get up and proceed with her day. She called Cante and agreed to meet her at the Mall of America in an hour.

*****

The Mall of America! The largest shopping mall in the United States. With over 550 different stores to choose from, one could find whatever they desired at the mall, located directly across the street from the international airport. The Mall of America was a thrill to see when you fly into Minnesota.

Erica pulled her Lexus coupe inside the Illinois parking section and was greeted by a huge replica of the Sears Tower.

After cruising through several lanes, she spotted Cante's Audi and parked alongside of it. Cante was talking on her phone, perched on the hood of her car. She was wearing Chanel frames and she had her hair pulled into a tight bun. As soon as Erica approached, she ended her call and the lecture began.

"I swear, you gone be late for your own funeral," she complained. Erica detected a hint of annoyance in her voice.

"Whatever happened to greeting a person with 'hello' or a hug and a kiss before giving them some attitude?" replied Erica while reaching and embracing Cante in a tight hug. She gave her a kiss on the cheek before pulling away and complimenting her.

"You look stunning this afternoon; your skin is glowing girl! I'm assuming that Steve is responsible for that?" she asked.

"Your compliments won't work this time, you had me waiting for over an hour, you stole whatever glow Steve did give me," complained Cante while pouting her lips.

"Ahh, you poor baby. I'm so sorry, come here and let mommy make it better," teased Erica while trying to embrace Cante in yet another hug. Cante took off running away from her toward the entrance of the mall as Erica gave chase. When she caught up, Cante was out of breath and laughing hysterically, "Okay, okay, I'm not mad anymore. But now I'm tired. I haven't run like that in months," said Cante, before grabbing ahold of Erica's hand, they entered the mall walking hand-in-hand.

As if they were in shopping heaven, every time they found a sense of solace while shopping. To Erica, this was her time just for herself, her own shangri-la. She worked every day in an effort to make other people's lives better, so she felt that she deserved one day to herself. After her split with Kyle, she had maxed out several credit cards while trying to block out everything that had transpired between them. Erica and Cante bounced back from store to store, purchasing everything that caught their eyes. Soon they found themselves in the handbag section of the Fendi store.

"What do you think about this one?" asked Cante as she checked out a clutch Fendi purse. "Do you think it goes well with the Louie heels?"

"Here let me see," said Erica as she took the handbag out of Cante hands. "Yes, this is a perfect match girl."

That was all the confirmation that Cante needed, and another twenty-five hundred dollars were charged to her card.

"I really like these frames right here; I think they bring out my eyebrows," Erica said as she modeled the shades for Cante.

"No, I think the all red ones fit you better," advised Cante before she sat down on the leather couch and poured herself another glass of champagne.

Being regular customers and spending large sums got you a complimentary bottle at Fendi. Erica made her way over to the shoes and grabbed a pair of heels that matched the red frames. She sat down next to Cante to try them on and was interrupted by security.

"Excuse me ladies, would one of you happen to be Erica Caldwell?" Cante looked at Erica questioningly.

"Yes, I'm Erica Caldwell, how may I help you?" she asked.

"Well, we've been sent to escort you back to the Jarred's Jewerly store that you two visited earlier," he said.

"Why? Is there a problem?" questioned Erica, she had concern written all over her face.

"I'm not sure, ma'am. I'm just following an order that was given to me. Please follow us.'

Erica looked at Cante, Cante had a horrified look on her face. They both got up, grabbed their bags and began to follow the security guards. Along the way, Cante leaned in and whispered in Erica's ear, "Girl, please tell me that you didn't shoplift out of these people's store!"

"Cante! Are you crazy? Of course, I didn't! Why would you even ask that?" Erica asked.

"One can never be too sure," replied Cante as they continued following their security escort. When they finally made it to the jewelry store, they were led to the manager. The security guard began to speak,

"This one here," he pointed with his finger toward Erica, "is Ms. Caldwell," he continued.

"Okay," replied the manager. "You gentlemen can leave now, your service is no longer necessary." The two security guards exited the store before Erica spoke, she said, "Can you please tell me what this is all about?"

"First, allow me to apologize for the way I had you summoned. Secondly, there was a special request for you because you have a gift waiting for you."

"A gift?" asked Erica.

"Yes, it's here in the back, if you would kindly give me a moment, I'll retrieve it." Once the manager exited, Cante spoke,

"I cannot wait to see what this is about."

Erica nodded her head in agreement as the manager returned with a black velvet box tied with a red bow. "May I please see your ID so that I can confirm your identity?" he asked. Erica showed him her ID and then was handed the jewelry box. She released the bow before opening it up, she gasped in surprise as her breath was stolen from her. Cante looked over at the piece and was taken aback. Before them sat an all platinum tennis bracelet wrapped in over one hundred flawless diamonds.

"Oh my!" said Erica. "Are you sure this is for me?"

"Of course, it was delivered specially for you. This piece here is one of a kind," the manager informed her.

"But who? I mean what? So how??.." Erica couldn't find the words to form her questions as she was stunned by the beauty of the piece.

The manager spoke again, "This piece was handcrafted and set to be delivered here to you. A gentleman came in earlier and asked for you to be escorted here to retrieve it."

"A gentleman? What was his name?" questioned Erica.

"Well, here's the thing, he gave strict orders that his identity be concealed," the manager reluctantly replied.

"Concealed?" questioned Erica. "Did he at least leave a message to be delivered with it?"

"No, actually he didn't. But what I will say is that whoever this gentleman was, he is quite fond of you."

Erica looked over at Cante before she began to speak.

"How much does a piece like this cost a person?"

"This particular piece was designed at a different location. It wasn't paid for here, but I could give you an estimate. I'd say that it cost somewhere between sixty and seventy-five thousand dollars."

"Sixty to seventy-five grand!? You have got to be kidding," shouted Cante and Erica in unison.

"Surely, I am not, it is somewhere in that range, there is no way to be one hundred percent certain. I wouldn't kid about something like that," the manager said with a confused look on his face.

"Oh my," Erica stated. "I cannot accept this; I know that my fiancée couldn't have purchased this. Something this expensive is not in our budget," she said, pushing the box back toward the manager. "You can take this back and please tell that gentleman, whoever he is, thanks but no thanks."

"I'm sorry Ms. Caldwell, but I cannot take this back. If you are trying to refund it, I can call our headquarters and get a statement of purchase for the purchase price and that amount can be refunded to you," he said.

"No, just take it back," Erica replied stubbornly.

"Girl, are you out yo mind?" interrupted Cante. "Here give it to me, I can accept it," added Cante reaching for the jewelry box. "And no, she's not trying to refund it. I'll talk some sense into her, don't you worry," Cante grabbed the box from the man and said, "thank you so much for your service, you have been an excellent help," and she yanked Erica away from the store.

*****

Thirty minutes later, Erica and Cante sat at a table at the Hibachi Bar and Grill. In the middle of their table sat the box containing the bracelet. It was open and on display while Cante and Erica discussed who it could've possibly come from. Cante had a look of complete concentration on her face while she listened to Erica. "I don't know. I mean there could only be a few possibilities. There aren't too many people that could afford to pay for a bracelet this expensive. The only person I could think of was Earl, but you said that he was already married, correct?"

"Yes, he's married. I seen the picture, they're happy," confirmed Cante. "Okay so let's go ahead and cancel him out. Now, there's the Spanish guy Sammy that owns the plaza on the north side. I know he still has a thing for me.

He actually asked me out on a date recently but of course I declined."

"Do you think he can afford it, that thing is really expensive?" Cante asked.

"Honestly, I know that he can, and this kind of thing is right up his alley. He had crossed my mind when the arrangement was sent to the office. I was going to contact him and ask did he send them but then I figured why open that can of worms if nothing could come of it."

"Okay, so you think the same person that sent the arrangements is the same person that purchased the bracelet?" asked Cante.

"That could be a possibility," replied Erica.

"Well, who is the other person that you believe could be responsible for all this?" asked Cante.

"Well, I don't even want to believe it could be this person..." Erica said as her words trailed off.

"Girl! Who? Spit it out" demanded Cante.

"The only other person that could have done this is Kyle," replied Erica with hesitation in her voice.

"Your Kyle?" questioned Cante.

"Yes, my old Kyle, but this doesn't really have his name written all over it."

"Why do you say that?"

Erica took her time before responding. It had been a couple of years since she had spoken openly of Kyle. He still was a touchy subject to her. "I mean, it's been three years and I haven't heard a word from him. Kyle is really stuck in his ways and he's really stubborn. He'd figure if I hadn't contacted him, why contact me. He knows that he hurt me way too much. He can't face me, that's why I haven't heard anything from him," Erica finished with a hint of pain in her voice.

"How do you know he hasn't changed and isn't seeking forgiveness?" asked Cante.

"That isn't possible, you'd have to know Kyle to understand," replied Erica.

"Well if it isn't Earl, Sammy, or Kyle, then who could it be?"

"Girl, I have no idea!"

Erica and Cante sat quietly as they went deep into thought. Erica grabbed the bracelet from the table and examined it. She had to admit it, it was really an elegant piece. Diamonds were indeed a girl's best friend. Whoever had this bracelet made knew her taste. This was something that she could see herself wearing. As much as she wanted to, she knew that she could not keep this.

There was no way she could explain such a purchase to Arnold. The thoughts of Arnold made her set the bracelet back into its box. "So, what are you thinking about?" asked Cante.

"How Arnold would kill me if I walked into the house with this on and no explanation as to where it came from," Erica said.

"Well," said Cante as she grabbed the bracelet out of the box and slipped it on her wrist, "you can always give it to me," she rationalized, giving Erica her best puppy dog's eyes.

"No, I cannot, but you can surely hold it until I figure out who I have to return it to."

"Okay," whined Cante. "But do we have to return it?"

"No, we don't have to return it, but I do," said Erica while laughing at her friend who sounded like a five-year-old being forced to return a lost puppy. Cante put the bracelet back into its box and stored it in her purse.

"So, what are you going to do now?" asked Cante.

"I don't know. Honestly, I'm just ready to pretend none of this is even happening," replied Erica before setting her head in the palms of her hands.

"Don't stress yourself out about it," replied Cante before continuing, "If something else mysterious happens, then we'll just have a private investigator look into it. Until then, we'll wait and see...just maybe our mystery man will show his face."

"Yeah, maybe...." replied Erica.

Chapter Seven

One month later...

The first day of June marked Erica's 35th birthday. Outside, the sky was clear, and the sun was shining. The snow had long ago melted and filtered down the drains, making way for bright green grass. Inside, Erica stepped out of the shower and twinkled her toes on the cold floor. She turned toward her full-length mirror attached to the wall before letting her towel slip from her body to the ground. Slowly, she began to examine herself from head to toe. She twirled around several times before facing herself again. She was 35 years young and still maintained her almost flawless appearance. She cupped her breasts into the palms of her hands and blew herself a kiss before stepping into the main bedroom. She walked inside her walk-in closet and began the process of searching for the perfect birthday attire. She had a good idea of what she would wear, she just enjoyed knowing all of the options were exhausted. She sat down Indian style on her closet floor and began going through all the pairs of heels, one by one. Her mind began drifting off to what the day could possibly have in store for her. She knew that Arnold was due back in town and would have something unique planned. She thought back to the previous year on this date and how he had flown her out to Paris unexpectedly. It wasn't her first trip to France, but it was her first time visiting in such a romantic way. During their trip, she was able to see how couples fell in love so easily while there. Before she had known that her feelings for Arnold were beginning to increase.

She had opened her mind to the idea of possibly allowing him into her heart. It had been close to two years of him patiently waiting. She reminisced on how they sailed the seas. While they were there the sun had reflected its light across the ocean. Leaving the sky the darkest orange, and the seas the melancholiest blue. She remembered feeling so at ease in his arms as he held her closely, leaning against the rails of the yacht. She had never expressed love to him before, she had never said those words even though he had told her time and time again. She looked up into his eyes and he kissed her soft and tenderly on the lips. She felt her heart skip a beat and held in the one tear that had done its best to escape from her eyes. She was terrified of the possibilities, but she felt it and she knew it, so she said it. He began to hold her close as if to protect her from whatever fears her heart held inside. Her words slowly replayed in his mind like the sweetest of melodies..."I love you too," he responded.

Ding dong.... Ding dong.... Ding dong...The sound of the doorbell broke Erica from her day dream. "Okay, here I come," she screamed while jumping to her feet. She grabbed hold of her robe and made her way down the stairwell to the door. "Who is it?" she asked, fastening her robe while opening the door. When the door slung open, there was no one before her. She took a step out toward the porch and looked around. Still no one. Weird, she thought before turning to head back inside. She looked down and noticed an envelope sitting on the pavement. She scooped it up and stepped inside, looked behind her toward the driveway once more to be sure that she didn't miss anyone. Satisfied, she closed the door behind her. She leaned her back against the door and began to open the envelope. Inside was a thick piece of stationary paper with her initials written in bold letters. She unfolded the letter (follow your heart for it is the one thing in which you cannot deceive. In a few hours a courier will be waiting to take you to your destination. Happy birthday!) it read. After reading the note, she folded it and smiled. "Okay Arnold, play your little game," she said and made her way back up the stairs to finish getting dressed.

*****

Two hours later, Erica sat at her vanity mirror while applying her finishing touches to her makeup. She guided the brush that was dabbed in mascara across her cheek once more. She then applied red lipstick to her pouty lips. "Perfect," she whispered as she stood up making her way over to the full-length mirror. There she stood looking as stunning as ever in all white, thigh high, Alexander McQueen dress with matching red and white Alexander McQueen heels. Her diamond earrings and necklace glistened as the diamonds danced in the light. She was pleased with her appearance and grabbed hold of her red Berkin bag before making her way back down the stairs.

Outside, she was greeted by a driver standing aside a black Lincoln town car.

"Hello Ms. Caldwell," he said while reaching to open the car's door. "I'll be your driver," he informed her. She climbed inside and looked around. there was another envelope sitting with a single red rose on top of it. She grabbed hold of the rose and brought it to her nose. She inhaled deeply and exhaled slowly, enjoying its sweet scent. She had always loved the smell of a freshly cut rose. She picked up the envelope and took out the letter that it held. She began to read: "Today is your special day! Sit back, relax and enjoy some wine as a day filled with surprise awaits you...Direct your driver to the Mississippi river front, there you'll find a horse a carriage and your king!"

"Where to?" asked the driver as he watched Erica finish reading the letter through the rearview mirror. "The river front of the Mississippi, sir," she replied before tossing the letter to the side. She grabbed herself a glass from the holder and pulled the bottle of wine from the ice-filled bucket. She poured herself a glass and took a gulp before leaning back gently against the leather cushioned seat.

What did he have up his sleeve this time? She pondered this as she looked at her ring finger and thought about the upcoming wedding date in December. Belize would be the destination. Marriage was one of those things she was never really certain about. A lifetime commitment to one person sort of frightened her. Could one person really love another faithfully forever? That was a question that she couldn't answer with any degree of certainty. She had never had a problem with holding up her end of a monogamous relationship, what frightened her the most was her partner's commitment to said relationship. Could a man really remain faithful and true, forever? She thought about her father and mother and how they'd been married for forty years. Growing up, she couldn't remember a time that they ever had separated. But did that mean that problems never existed? Or were they just really good at concealing those problems?

She thought back to her and Arnold. She had never had an argument with him. He had never disrespected her or even taken her from granted. But what about 20 years from now? What would happen if she began to change physically and just wasn't quite as appealing to him as she was now. Would he still remain faithful? Could he still remain faithful? She glanced out the window and watched as they passed leafy trees that were barren only a month prior. Oh, how this world has its funny ways of changing she thought to herself. She also reminisced on how just three years ago she was left heartbroken, lost, and alone in this world just like the branches on the trees during the winter. Now she felt loved, complete, and fulfilled like the trees that were filled with leaves in the spring.

He will love me forever she thought. "We shall be arriving at the river front in moments," the driver interrupted her thoughts. Erica sat up and began to look out the window toward the waters of the Mississippi.

"I'll tell you when to stop," she replied. She continued looking out the window and she thought back to the message: "There you'll find a horse, a carriage, and a king..." the words replayed in her head. They drove down the trail and watched as people sailed, fished, and just sat idle while overlooking the river and enjoying its vastness and beauty. In the distance, Erica could see what appeared to be an all-white and gold carriage attached by reigns to two white thoroughbred horses. "Stop right here, please," she directed the driver. He pulled up alongside the trail. The driver got out and made his way to her door to open it. Erica exited and took in the breeze that came off the river, it chilled her skin. She inhaled the aroma and took in the scenery. "Amazing," she thought. She began walking toward the carriage. She approached and made her way to the front toward the horses. She got closer and noticed him for the first time with his back to her slowly stoking the silky coat of the horse with his hand.

"There you are," she said. "Where did you get a horse and carriage from?" He wore an off-white Armani vest that hugged up to his muscular back. His slacks were being held up by suspenders and the gold trimming of his Stacy Adam's shined brightly against the white leather they were made of. She walked closer before he began to speak.

"I bought this horse and carriage only a month ago," he said, turning to face her.

"Kyle!!" she whispered in shock.

*****

"Who did you expect?" asked Kyle while walking toward her. Erica stood frozen in her tracks. A rush of emotions flooded her all at once. How could this be? She hadn't seen or heard from him in over three years. Tears began to stream down her face and hands covered her mouth. She tried to take a step back but couldn't seem to move.

"You shouldn't be crying on your birthday," he said with a smirk. He got closer and pulled her into his arms. He breathed in the delightful scent of her perfume. He held her tighter like he would lose her if he didn't. She stood frozen within his embrace. She heard herself ask him to let go of her, but the words never came. She couldn't control her thoughts, her body, or the chill that swept through it. Kyle took a step back, allowing their bodies to separate. He used his thumb to brush away her hair that the wind blew in her face. He looked down into her eyes, "You are still as beautiful as I remember you," he said.

"What are you doing here Kyle?" she asked coldly, finally able to speak.

"I'm here to wish you a happy birthday and I was sort of hoping you would take a ride with me so I could finally explain myself."

"You should have tried explaining yourself three years ago," she replied before quickly turning to walk away. Kyle gently grabbed hold of her hand, stopping her from proceeding any further. She turned to face him and before he knew it, she brought her hand up and slapped him quickly across the face.

"How dare you turn up here after three years and act as if nothing happened? Three years, Kyle! I gave you nineteen years of my life and you didn't have the decency to give me an explanation. You hurt me and then went about your life as if I never meant a thing to you." Tears began to roll down her cheeks. She had thought that these feelings were gone. She had told herself that she had forgotten it all, but all at once her emotions took hold.

"I couldn't face you, Erica. I know that it isn't a good enough reason and I admit that I was a coward. I couldn't stand to see the hurt in your eyes, especially since I was the cause of it. I haven't been able to go forward. Three years and I've been hurting as well, it wasn't just you. I never went about my life because once you left, life as I knew it stopped." Silence invaded the space between them. Kyle looked down at his feet. He looked back up and spoke again. "I've been holding this pain in my chest for years and I need to get it out just as much as you need to hear me out. I just need one minute of your time," he begged. She heard the sincerity in his voice. She looked deeper into his eyes. Here stood the man that had introduced her into womanhood. The man that had taught her the ways of the world. The one that had once protected her, cared for her, and cherished her. He was also the man that had brought another woman into their home.

"I can't," she replied before beginning to walk back to the town car. Kyle kept pace with her and began to speak.

"When will I have a chance to explain myself? he asked.

"You won't," she firmly replied. "I've moved on with my life and refuse to slow it down by revisiting the past."

"How can you revisit a place that you never left?" he asked. "Your eyes have always given you away, Erica. You haven't changed, they still give you away. You knew that it wasn't him sending you all those gifts." His words caused her to temporarily pause. "Just like deep down you knew he wasn't the one leading you here today."

Erica stopped as she stood aside the town car. The driver made his way toward her door. Kyle took a step forward and in front of her, narrowing their distance.

"You knew that we were going to be meeting from the moment you picked up that letter this morning. You have always noted that I have a distinguished style of writing. Even with you knowing all of this, you still showed up today."

She looked down at the ground because her eyes would betray her. "I waited here because I told myself that if you showed, your heart has been longing for me just as mine had been longing for you. You've followed your heart because it is the one thing in which you cannot deceive." Kyle paused briefly as Erica took this all in. "I'm not here for you to tell me that you forgive me in one day. I'm not here to tell you to stop living the life that you have been living. But what I am telling you is that I want you back. I spent nineteen years of my life to get you to love me once, and I'm willing to spend the rest of it to get you to love me again." He stepped aside, allowing the driver to open the door for Erica. She climbed inside and looked back out at him once more before the driver closed the door. He made his way to the driver's side and slowly got in. He pulled away from the curb back toward Erica's house. Kyle placed his hand in the pockets of his slacks and let out a defeated sigh. He watched as the car made its way down the trail, taking the love of his life away from him once again.

Chapter Eight

Kyle sat at the head of the conference table, joining him was Alu, Mr. Collins, and two representatives of the Chinese banking firm in which they were in negotiations. They were currently in the mists of a heated discussion concerning certain investments that were underperforming.

Mr. Collins and the World National Bank had huge interest in the Chinese firm and had become concerned, so they brought in Alu and Kyle to help assist in figuring it out.

"Currently, there is over 100 million tied into the bond department of our portfolio," began Alu, "the problem is that the bond market has been underperforming for quite some time now and the strategy that we have in place has proven to be inefficient. The flow of investment funds is going elsewhere as you can see." Alu pointed at the projection screen containing spreadsheets and graphs outlining performance in their portfolio's bonds.

"Yes, we see that funds are currently flowing toward the housing market, but what point are we trying to make?" asked the Chinese rep.

"The housing market is booming and is on pace to continue for at least the next five to seven years. This is where I feel the solution to our problem lies. I propose that we remove 50 million from bonds and place them into home loan programs to keep pace with the competition."

The Chinese rep cut in, "The housing market seems promising but what happens if that bubble suddenly bursts? With too much invested in these markets we could, potentially, lose millions."

"Responsible lending prevents that," remarked Kyle.

"Statistics show that the housing market isn't likely to fall for at least the next five years. Now is the time to relocate those funds, that's the only way we'll be able to keep up with our competitors," said Alu.

"I believe it to be extremely risky to remove 50 million that's giving us 3% guaranteed and place it into a volatile market. I understand the potential but it's a preposterous suggestion," argued the Chinese rep.

"No, what's preposterous is leaving it to gain 3% when we can be gaining an extra 4% in a stronger market. The numbers and the direction of the economy says it makes perfect sense," Kyle stated with irritation in his voice.

"We already have an excess of over 200 million tied up in home loans across the globe. Why would we add more when history has shown us the housing market can suddenly turn for the worse?" reminded the Chinese rep.

The room became quite and extremely tense as the discussion continued. "When it comes down to it, we have two possibilities that are legitimate options. We can leave the funds as they are and continue to under-perform or we can pull out and relocate. Home loans aren't the only option; student loans are bringing 5% and we can evenly split the take between the two. Diversify and lessen your risk, it's ECON 101," Kyle said patronizingly.

The Chinese rep stood up from his chair and began pacing the floor. He had a look of agitation on his face. He said, "'There is a reason we've survived so long in the banking industry and based on speculation is not it. You are simply thinking short term, we have to continue being wise in our decision-making process so that we can stay strong in the upcoming century. Our current strategy ensures that."

"Your strategy also ensures that you will continue losing standing and position if you fail to adapt to the economy. Your strategy is outdated. If you want to be around for the centuries to come you have to change it or we will be forced here again, in the future, to help fix this mess," yelled Alu at the Chinese rep with equal agitation.

"Arrogance has led to the fall of many men," responded the Chinese rep.

"Arrogance has nothing to do with the matter. I would think a man of your caliber and in your position would understand the flow of the investment world, but clearly, you don't. Cause and effect, supply and demand, these are simple principles," replied Alu with a pitch in his voice.

"Okay, okay, gentlemen. Let's calm down a second," interrupted Mr. Collins. "We're not here to have a pissing contest. Apparently, Mr. Francis has a point; if our strategy was efficient, we wouldn't be here having these discussions today. The purpose of the meeting is to find a solution. Currently, we have better performing assets within our portfolio that we can increase our positions in by removing the funds from the bonds. This seems to be the most rational solution. Now, once we remove the funds, we have to establish a plan that will allow us to gain our position back within the bond market once it recovers. So, lets figure out a way to make this possible," finished Mr. Collins. The room became quiet again as the meeting's attendees glanced at one another fearfully. Finally, Kyle began to speak.

"The bond market is set to recover in about five years, lets remove 50 million and strategically place it in the home and student loans. In about four years we should have turned the 50 million into 100 million. We'll then place the 50 million back into bonds right in time. With this strategy, we keep pace with our competitors without losing standing in the market," Kyle finished and looked, triumphantly, around the room. The Chinese reps began hesitantly displaying their approval and Alu winked at Kyle. Mr. Collins began to speak again.

"I believe we have our solution then, gentlemen. Let's end discussions there. Thank you, gentlemen, for your input," he ended.

The attendees stood and began shaking hands. Kyle exited the conference room followed by Alu and Mr. Collins. They entered the lobby and sat down on the adjacent couches before taking deep breaths in and out. Kyle's stress levels always seemed to peak in overseas meetings.

"Man, I hope those guys begin to open their minds to rationality, Alu, "if you don't continually adapt, you'll eventually get left by the wayside, in this new world of investing."

"They'll understand eventually, and if they don't, they'll soon find themselves out of a job," responded Mr. Collins.

"I'm just glad this is over with. Boy, I'm ready to get back to the states," said Kyle. "I enjoy Singapore, but I cannot get used to it."

"The feeling is certainly mutual," replied Mr. Collins. He got up and gave himself a quick stretch. "The jet should be ready to depart in a little over an hour. I have a couple of loose ends to tie up with these gentlemen in here and then I'll be ready to depart," finished Mr. Collins before walking back into the conference room.

Kyle pulled out his cell phone and noticed that he had several missed calls. Big Momma was responsible for a few, being that she had a phobia of flying and would call several times in order to check on his safety. He smiled at the thought of the old woman. At times, she still treated him like a child. The other missed call he had was from Lou.

He hadn't talked to him since his encounter with Erica. He figured Lou would be trying to see how it all played out. Even though Lou was known to handle things differently within his encounters with a woman, he understood his friend and admired his faith in love.

Kyle glanced down at his Rolex and figured them to be asleep at this hour. His body had not yet adjusted to the time difference, he stood up, yawned and stretched.

"I'm going to make my way down to the limo. Alu, my body is shutting down on me. I'll see you when you make it down."

"Alright, old man," Alu quipped while looking down at his smartphone.

Kyle made his way to the elevator and descended the sixty floors to his awaiting limo. He climbed inside, got comfortable and shut his eyes.

"Okay then, if you love me like you say you do, give me five reasons why" said Erica.

"Only five? That's easy. One, because you are easily the prettiest girl on campus. Two, because you always make me laugh. Three, your lips taste like bubble gum. Four, I can talk to you about anything and five is because you love me," he finished.

"Wait a minute, you can't use because I love you as a reason," Erica complained.

"Why not? That's a legit reason."

"How is that silly?"

"Because if you don't love me, how could I possibly love you?"

"No, you have to give me a better reason, the fifth one doesn't count," said Erica stubbornly while looking at Kyle in anticipation.

"Okay, let me see, the fifth reason why I love you is because you have always had a way of making me feel like I'm the only guy in the world," Kyle finished before putting his arm around her.

"Do you really mean these things?" she asked.

"Of course, if I didn't, I wouldn't have said them." Kyle brought Erica closer to him, "Besides, I must really love you if I deal with you snoring like a bulldog every time afterwards."

"Not true," said Erica while pushing herself away from him.

"So true. If only you could hear yourself'." Kyle began imitating the sound that bulldogs make while snoring.

"Shut up." Erica got up and quickly jumped on top of him. She cradled his body before he picked her up and tossed her over his shoulder. He began playfully spinning her around in circles.

"Stoooopppp," she screamed while laughing, "put me down," she demanded.

"Say that I'm the king and that I rule the entire universe," he replied while spinning.

"Heyyy, you two, what are you doing in there?" screamed their roommate. Kyle dumped Erica back on top of his bed and climbed alongside of her. He scooted closer to her while looking into her eyes.

"You see, you are going to get us both into trouble," said Erica with a devilish grin. He scooted even closer to her and kissed her on her lips. They both lay back in bed and continued to kiss. Erica could feel her body heating up as Kyle slipped his tongue into her mouth.

"I'm really about to get us into trouble now."

She let out a soft moan when he began kissing her on the neck. He sucked her with just the right amount of pressure as she gasped continuously. She reached and began pulling at his shirt and pulled it over his head, he raised his body allowing for it to come off. He went down and slipped his tongue into her mouth again. He softly grinded his body firmly between her legs. She wrapped them around his waist, enjoying the friction. He pulled away and began kissing her neck and moved down to her collar bone. He then moved down, passing softly over the cups of her bra and down to her stomach. She gasped while rubbing her hands over his head. He whispered her name softly, lightly pecking her soft skin with tender kisses. He slowly began unbuckling her jeans. He began gentle kissing the inside of her thighs. He kissed his way back up, briefly stopping at her crotch and softly biting through the fabric. He could imagine the taste as he lifted her up and began removing her jeans...

Kyle abruptly woke from his dream. He felt himself sweating about the forehead and underneath his suit. He looked around, completely disoriented, trying to figure out where he was. He saw that they were pulling up to the company jet at the airstrip. He turned and caught Mr. Collins' eye. "How was your nap?" asked Mr. Collins with a knowing smirk on his face. Kyle looked from Mr. Collins to Alu who was also smirking. "So who is Erica?" asked Mr. Collins before Alu broke into laughter.

Chapter Nine

"Man, does it feel good to be back home!" Kyle said, while leaning back on Big Momma's couch. He had his tie loosened and a Corona in hand, he felt as if he were about to explode after gorging himself on Big Momma's cooking.

"It sure feels good to have you back home chilli. I've been missing you ever since you left. When are you going to come back home for good?" asked Big Momma.

"When I become complete again," said Kyle sadly.

"And how long might that take?"

"That doesn't solely depend on me."

"Chilli, I don't understand it, but whenever you get done speaking in riddles just know that you are missed and wanted here."

"I know, Big Momma, hopefully it won't take that long."

"What are you two talking about?" asked Lou as he entered the living room while taking off his jacket. He arrived late as usual.

"Hey chilli. What took you so long to get here?" asked Big Momma incredulously.

She got up and made her way over to Lou. Lou reached down and hugged her before giving her a kiss on the forehead.

"Traffic was horrendous out there!" he lied.

"What's up Lou?" asked Kyle from the couch. "You are about an hour late; I didn't think that you was coming so I went ahead and ate your portion," finished Kyle while making a show of rubbing his stomach.

"Big Momma, please tell me you didn't let him eat my food."

"Of course, not Louis, don't let him worry you. I'll go warm it up for you right now, everything but the collard greens, right?"

"You still remember," replied Lou before taking a seat on the couch.

"How can I forget? I have been feeding you ever since you were twelve years old." Big Momma made her way into the kitchen as Kyle and Lou began to talk.

"So how did your meeting in China turn out?"

"It was rather tense actually. We sat down with two reps from the Chinese firm and tried putting together a new investment strategy that will allow us to keep pace with the competition. You wouldn't believe that they've been following the same strategy for twenty years," boasted Kyle.

"Twenty years of the same practices? How can they possibly expect to keep up with competing banks? Did it all get figured out?" asked Lou.

"Yeah, after debating for over two hours. You wouldn't believe they referred to us as arrogant," Kyle laughed as he thought back on the conversation.

"The humble Kyle arrogant, huh?" Lou laughed briefly at the suggestion. "If they thought you were arrogant then they would really hate me. You know I just wrapped up a 140-million-dollar contract with a distribution conglomerate in Japan. An easy 35 million for four years."

"Yeah, go ahead and brag. So how much does that bring your annual earnings to?"

"If I told you then you would really think that I was bragging. But just know, imma be rich forever, and ever and ever oh oh oh oh, imma be rich forever," sang Lou as he imitated the popular rap lyrics.

Kyle began to laugh at his friend. Even though Lou bragged at times, he knew Lou had worked really hard to get to this point in his life. He had stepped outside the boundaries of traditional finance and took an extraordinary risk when he turned down becoming the CEO of another major distribution conglomerate in order to start his own. The risk had paid off in more ways than one. Everyone told him he was crazy for trying and when he succeeded, he laughed in all their faces and counted his money. He now had one of the top five distribution chains on the SNP 500.

"No, but seriously, I'm trying to hear about Erica's reaction when she seen you in front of that horse and carriage," said Lou animatedly.

"How do you even know she showed up?" asked Kyle rhetorically.

"Because if she didn't you would still be there plotting and there is no doubt in my mind that she is still in love with you in the same way that you are with her. I'm just trying to figure out what happened when she did show up?" said Lou.

"Yeah, she did show up, but it didn't go too well, she slapped me and then left." Kyle looked toward the kitchen to make sure this last part hadn't been overheard.

"Hold up, she slapped you?" Kyle just shook his head affirmatively.

"You deserved that, the slapping part, not the leaving part, that is. So, did she say anything whatsoever?"

"She said that she moved on and didn't have time to be going backwards. But of course, you and I know better. I mentioned the gifts, but I didn't really get a reaction to either. She just gave me her patented 'you figured me out' look. I told her I want her back and that I'm going to do whatever in order to get her back. She's still hurting bro and that's understandable."

"Yeah, we both know that you didn't handle that situation correctly back then. So, how did she look after all that time? Has she changed much?" inquired Lou.

"She was beautiful, she took my breath away, just like she used to. She was wearing an all-white thigh-high dress; her hair was down, and her lips were looking good." Kyle paused briefly to shake his head in astonishment.

"Damn," he said to himself as his chin slumped into his chest.

"Damn, bro, but look at the bright side, she wore that just for you."

"Yeah, I thought about that too," said Kyle.

"Thought about what?" asked Big Momma as she came into the living room carrying a platter of food and a pitcher of Kool-Aide. She walked over and handed them to Lou. Before repeating "thought about what, Kyle?" Kyle sat quietly while thinking of a response. He tried getting Lou's attention so he could divert the conversation from him, but Lou was busy stuffing his mouth with food. The silence stood before Lou finally looked up and began to speak.

"He was saying that he thought about what Erica wore for him when he seen her." Big Momma looked at Kyle with a questioning look on her face. Kyle looked over at Lou and shook his head.

"Oh," said Lou while studying Big Momma. "I'm assuming you didn't know?" Lou looked back and forth between the two.

Big Momma kept her eyes fixed on Kyle while awaiting his explanation.

"I was going to tell you when I got her back," said Kyle and still staring at Lou angrily.

"What bro? How was I supposed to know that you didn't tell her?"

"So that's where you've been these past couple of months?" asked Big Momma.

"Yes, I was tired of wondering and tired of sleepless nights. My days were becoming long and my nights even longer. I'm trying to get her back Big Momma, before it's too late."

"That's what you supposed to do chilli. Sometimes we get ourselves so caught up into living life that we forget that we don't have forever to live it. You have to go after what you want while you can because there is no telling when it will be over," Big Momma spoke with the wisdom of nearly a century on this Earth. She then shifted her attention to Lou, "So Louis when are you going to find you a nice young lady to settle down with?"

"Huhm?" mumbled Lou with a mouthful of food, pretending to have not heard Big Mamma.

"You heard correctly," said Kyle trying to put the pressure on someone else. "She said when are you going to find yourself a nice young lady to settle down with?"

Lou looked over at Kyle and couldn't help but smirk. He knew that Kyle was trying to get him back for spilling the beans earlier. Lou grabbed his glass of Kool-Aide and washed his food down before speaking. "As long as I have Big Momma, there's no need for another woman in my life."

"Chilli, you been using that same line since you were twenty-five. You need to find yourself a nice young lady that compliment you. Either that or you need to find yourself a new line," Big Momma joked. "But seriously baby, there is nothing like having a partner to share this journey with. You have to know that love is one of the Lord's greatest blessings to Man and one that you should be trying your hardest to enjoy."

"Yeah, I know Big Momma. Maybe he will bless me to experience it one day," Lou said seriously.

Big Momma, Lou, and Kyle sat for hours talking about life, their careers, and the mysteries of love. Both Lou and Kyle looked forward to talks with Big Momma because they always felt much wiser afterward. Big Momma was something of a sage in matters of finding true love. She had been married to Poppa Malone since the tender age of eighteen. He was her first and only love. They had been through the trials and tribulations of making a marriage work. They had done so through times of social injustice and societies hardships. Big Momma and Poppa Malone had stayed strong and loved each other through it all. Big Momma still ached silently every day at the departure of her one true soul mate.

As the night grew late, Big Momma got up and made her way toward the stairs. "I don't have it the way I used to chilli, I'm going to make my way to bed. Kyle, you make sure that you clean the dishes and lock up."

"Okay Big Momma, thank you for the meal and I love you," replied Kyle.

"Yeah, thank you Big Momma and I love you too," chimed Lou.

"You are welcome chilli and of course I love ya'll as well," said Big Momma as she made her way off to bed.

"I'm about to call it one too, when are you headed back to Minnesota?" asked Lou while getting up to put on his jacket.

"In a few days. I have an important meeting with Mr. Swiss and then after that, I'm going to head on back."

"Well, I'm trying to make it back that way with you. It's been quite some time since I've visited the Twin Cities. I'm sure I have a lady friend or three that I can contact. I'll have to pull out my little black book."

Kyle shook his head at Lou. He wondered himself if Lou would ever find that one. Lou had always said that he couldn't find a woman who would keep up with him. Kyle knew that eventually he'd find his kryptonite.

"Alright that's a bet bro, drive safe."

Chapter Ten

"Hey girl,'" Cante greeted, answering Erica's call.

"Hey," Erica said unenthusiastically.

"What's the matter with you?" Cante wondered.

"I need someone to talk to, where are you?"

"I'm coming through the international airport now. I forgot to tell you that Steve flew me out to the Virgin Islands for the week, I'm just now getting home."

"Virgin Islands, huh? You and Steve must be getting serious."

"More like not. Steve's cool and it was nice, but it will be our last time seeing one another," stated Cante matter-of-factly.

"Why is that? He seems really nice," asked Erica, curious.

"You know I have rules girl. You get two chances to sweep me off my feet, if you cannot do that, then I'm moving along."

"Don't you think it takes more than two dates to decide if you want to be with a person?"

"It only takes two. I know what I want and sorry, but Steve is not it. Let's not waste precious time discussing my past, tell me what you need to talk about."

Erica became quiet before she responded. "Girl, my world has been a complete mess over the past couple of weeks. It seems to be getting progressively worse. I finally found out who was sending me all those expensive gifts."

"Really? What is taking you so long to tell me?"

"It was Kyle."

"How did you find out?"

"He showed up on my birthday."

"Wait a minute, your birthday was two weeks ago. Why am I just now hearing about this?"

"Because, I'm just now feeling up to talking about it. Anyway, he left a note that directed me to the river front. Initially, I thought it was Arnold, but when I arrived Kyle was there."

"Okay, so what happened?"

"He asked me for an opportunity to explain himself. During his explanation he made it clear that he is so arrogant he believed I would fall right into his arms. Girl, I ended up giving him a firm slap across his face for the audacity he showed. Then, I tried leaving but he stopped me, saying that he is going to do anything to get me back."

"So, what did Arnold have to say about all this?" questioned Cante with concern.

"I haven't told Arnold."

"Now I'm really confused. Kyle is in town and has not only been sending gifts but has popped up and you haven't told Arnold?"

"No," Erica replied guiltily.

"Okay, then there's got to be more to all this. I'm listening." Cante gave a look that said, 'go on.' She knew her friend had to be in a difficult position.

"Honestly, a part of me felt that it's been Kyle all along. The day of my birthday I felt it was him leading me to the river front. Or I just wanted it to be him. Now, I know all of this may sound crazy considering my circumstances with Arnold. But for the life of me I can't explain why Kyle has been on my mind constantly." Cante sat quietly and listened because she knew Erica wasn't finished yet.

"I feel so bad Cante because Arnold has been so good to me and he doesn't deserve me keeping secrets from him."

"So, what are you planning to do because nothing good will come from keeping secrets, especially one as big as this."

"I really don't know girl. I guess I'll have to be firm next time and let Kyle know that I have no plans on letting him back into my life."

"Are you sure that's what you want to do?"

"Not really..."

"Yeah, this is messy," replied Cante.

"Tell me about it," Erica replied with sadness in her voice.

"Come on now, I cannot stand to hear you sounding like that. Where are you and where's Arnold?"

"I'm at home and Arnold just left for New York for business."

"Then we need to get you out of that house. You are in no condition to be laying around. You will just sit there and sulk. There's a celebration going on at Aqua's tonight, come out with me girl. Just you and me. No men, no worries, and no distractions. We'll get it all figured out once we get you loosened up a little bit."

"I don't know Cante, I'm in no mood for the club."

"Yes, you are. I'll be by your place at 11 p.m. Don't leave me hanging."

Cante ended the conversation before Erica could protest any more.

Aqua was full of energetic people on this warm, Friday night. Erica and Cante were in the mix, dancing freely to the pounding music. Erica's hands were held high in the air and her hips swayed to the beat as she danced. The glimmer from her tight red Versace dress reflected in the dark club. Cante was close by Erica's side, matching her rhythm. Her black Ferragamo skirt rosé dangerously up her long legs, giving the men dancing alongside her plenty to enjoy.

They danced with the men for several songs as the multi-colored lights cased through the club. Cante felt herself becoming extremely hot, so she decided to exit the dance floor.

She headed back over to their VIP booth and took a sip of her dolce. Less than a minute later she noticed Erica heading her way.

"How are you gonna leave me out there with two complete strangers?" asked Erica angrily as she slid into the booth next to Cante'.

"I'm sorry but I was getting too hot. I couldn't take it."

"You are losing it girl, you used to be able to dance for hours," teased Erica.

"I still can go for hours; I just have to be with a sexy man."

"Are sex and men the only things that motivate you?"

"First off, I said sexy and of course not girl, you forgot to mention money," Cante corrected her, completely serious. Erica couldn't help but laugh at her friend's bluntness, it was something that she had always admired about her. She was still laughing as a waiter made her way to their table, she placed a bottle of Ace of Spades on their table.

"I'm sorry Ms. but we didn't order this," announced Cante.

"This bottle was sent over compliments of the gentlemen seated over there," said the waitress as she pointed off in the direction of a separate VIP booth. She then handed Cante a note that simply stated, "The pleasure is all mine, beautiful."

Cante glanced over at the booth the waitress was talking about and she examined the light skinned man wearing a fitted black and green Louis Vuitton V-Neck. He was holding a bottle of Belair Rose in his hand while nodding his head slowly to the music. She watched as he took a sip before licking his lips. His diamond-studded earrings and bracelet aluminized its own light throughout the club.

"Can you please tell him that he should've brought it over himself like a real gentleman," she returned the bottle to the waitress.

"Of course," replied the waitress with a smile. She made her way back to the handsome man's booth and Cante watched the surprised expression on his face followed by a slight smirk. He tipped back his champagne again, allowing the waitress to depart. A few seconds later, the man got up and headed his way toward their section.

"Girl, I hope you don't have no crazy man popping up over here."

"Don't worry, I'll be the one dealing with it. That ring on your finger will scare him away don't worry," joked Cante.

"Here he comes now," observed Erica.

"They always come," replied Cante.

"You are a conceited ass."

"No, my ass is confident."

They watched as the man waded through the crowd and approached their booth. As he got closer, he began to look familiar to Erica. He had a confident swagger and a walk that said he owned the ground he walked on. When he approached he smiled, revealing pearly white teeth.

After noticing Erica his smile began to widen. They did know one another. "Oh my god, how are you? What are you doing here Louis? It's been such a long time!" Erica screamed as she got up to embrace Louis in a hug. At that moment, Cante stood to make her presence known. "Louis, this is my best friend Cante, Cante this is Louis, a childhood friend." Cante extended her hand toward Louis as the introductions were being finished.

"I'm sorry, but I prefer hugs," stated Louis smoothly, before reaching in and embracing her.

The smell of his cologne ignited something deep within her and she felt those places moisten. As he pulled away, he let his lip brush her neck. "A peach," he noted to himself while lustfully eyeing her.

"Excuse me?" said Cante who didn't hear what he said.

"Never mind," he replied.

"Louis, what are you doing here in Minnesota?" asked Erica.

"Actually, I'm here visiting a very close friend of mine, I'm sure that you know him," he replied, before turning back toward his VIP booth. He made a gesture, waving his accomplice over, before turning back to face the ladies. Erica tried looking around him to see who it was he was waving over. As the man approached, she felt a lump form in her throat. At that moment, Kyle appeared causing her to stiffen up and glare disapprovingly at him.

Cante this is Kyle, my best friend. Kyle, this is Cante" Cante reached out and shook Kyle's hand."

"I've heard a lot about you!" she stated before looking over at Erica.

"So, do the two of you mind if we join you or are you already expecting company?" asked Lou mischievously.

"Of course, we don't mind," blurted Cante. Erica shot her a look and if it could kill, it would have struck her dead on the spot. Cante gave her a sneaky little smile and shrugged her shoulders before scooting over, making room for Louis in the booth next to her.

"May I?" asked Kyle to Erica, joining her in the booth before she could answer. She rolled her eyes as he slid in next to her.

"I guess I don't have any choice in the matter," she retorted.

"What are you doing here?" she asked angrily. "I'm out showing a friend a good time, why? Is that a crime?"

"No, it's not a crime but if I believed in coincidence, I still wouldn't believe that you just happened to be here," replied Erica, giving him a knowing look.

"Are you trying to insinuate that I'm a stalker?" Kyle asked, obviously offended.

"No, I prefer the term 'calculating.'"

"In that case, you really should believe in coincidence," replied Kyle.

Erica gave him a questioning look but didn't reply right away. She glanced over at Lou and Cante, seeing Lou whispering in her ear.

Cante leaned her head back and laughed at whatever Lou was whispering.

"You really are blunt, aren't you?" Cante observed.

"That's the only way to be," replied Lou before waving his hand to get the passing waitress' attention. "Excuse me, Miss, we are trying to place some drink orders," he said.

The waitress stopped to take their orders. "What are ya'll drinking tonight?" Lou asked Cante.

"I'm having Patron," responded Cante.

"Okay, so can we get two fifths of Patron, 3 Belair gold bottles, a bottle of Dom and... what are you drinking, Erica?" Lou paused to ask.

"She will have a bottle of Dolce," Kyle answered before she could say anything. When Erica didn't protest Lou continued, "we'll also have a bottle of Dolce, please."

The waitress left to go fill their orders. Kyle leaned into Erica and began to whisper in her ear.

"If I didn't know any better, I'd say you were disappointed to see me."

"I wouldn't say I'm disappointed, but I wouldn't say that I'm thrilled either," Erica stubbornly replied.

"I can accept that, even though, I must admit, it feels really good to see you. You are looking really good I must add."

"Please keep your compliments to yourself, I have a fiancée who wouldn't appreciate it."

"I could care less about your fiancée," Kyle replied arrogantly. "Besides, I never knew an engagement had to be permanent."

"It isn't, the marriage that follows it is."

"Well, let's talk about him if that happens. For now, I'm trying to talk about you and how that dress compliments you."

Again, she didn't reply. She turned her head just in time to see the waitress approaching with their drinks. After the drinks were placed on the table, Lou grabbed ahold of the Patron bottles and popped them open. He poured a glass for Cante while Kyle imitated him and poured some Dolce for Erica.

The foursome sat sipping the variety of potables that sat in front of them and listened to the music playing in the club. Cante seemed to really be enjoying Lou's company. She was laughing constantly at his every word and couldn't seem to keep her hands off him.

Erica found herself feeling slightly uncomfortable in Kyle's presence. It had been such a long time since she had been around him in such close proximity.

She found herself feeling a rush of different emotions all at once. After the liquor began taking effect, she loosened up just a little. She looked over at Kyle as he held a bottle of Blaire in his hand and nodded to the music. Man was he handsome and nicely dressed. The Polo by Ralph Lauren Red Cologne he was wearing aroused her more than she cared to admit.

"Get it together, girl" she said to herself before scooting away from him just a little.

"So, Erica, how's Minnesota been treating you?" asked Lou.

"Actually, it has been pretty good. I've been running my non-profit and just taking everything else day by day."

"That's wonderful, but I must admit, Chicago really misses you. Are you planning on coming back anytime soon?" Lou questioned.

"I'm not sure, there are just too many bad memories left there. Minnesota has been much more peaceful on the mind and body."

Lou made a face that conveyed he caught the apparent shot thrown in his friend's direction.

"I'm sorry to hear that, but believe it or not, you are really missed back home," he said sincerely.

"Yeah, you are," Kyle added as Erica looked his way.

"I'm sure she knows that," interrupted Cante before she continued, "enough about Chicago. We are here live at Aqua's. The music is off the chain and so are the men." She lustfully eyed Lou after the statement.

"The women are off the chain this evening, too," replied Lou.

"Well, I say we stop talking and hit the dance floor. Patron makes me want to dance," finished Cante before she took another sip of her drink.

"Is that all Patron makes you want to do?" Lou asked seductively.

"Maybe and maybe not. Let's hit the dance floor and we can figure out what else it makes me want to do after that." She placed her hand on Lou's lap under the table before sliding her way out the booth and headed toward the dance floor.

"Slow down a little," yelled Lou as he hurried out of the booth behind her following her out to the dance floor.

Erica and Kyle remained inside the booth. It felt weird to Erica being alone with him.

"I see you still enjoy the club scene," Kyle said trying to break the ice and the barrier Erica had built up.

"Cante asked me to come out with her so I figured why not enjoy some music and dance."

"Why aren't you dancing then?"

"I'm no longer in the mood."

"Don't tell me I'm the cause of that."

Erica gave him a glare but didn't respond. She didn't want to give him any leeway. She wanted to feel the distance he had caused three years ago. He knew that she was being stubborn, acting like she didn't want to be bothered. He enjoyed the chase and didn't have plans on allowing her to run him off. He knew her triggers better than anyone else and he knew ways to break down the barriers she had built. Kyle took another gulp of his drink. "I didn't come out tonight to be a sitting duck. Imma hit the floor. I would love for you to join me, I'm sure it will be better than sitting here alone. Half drunk and pouting."

"I'm not pouting," she spat.

"I'm saying are you going to join me, or what?" Kyle asked while sliding out of the booth, extending a hand to her. She looked at his hand without any intention of accepting it.

Part of her was screaming no but there was another part, in the back of her mind that was rationalizing 'it's only dancing.'

"Please, don't try anything extra," she replied, accepting his hand. They made it out to the floor and caught the rhythm of the song playing. Kyle looked down on her as they danced. The feeling made him reminisce on the time they were together. They visited just about every club in and outside of the city of Chicago. They did it just to relish in the mood and dance.

Kyle brought his body back into hers, trying to feel that familiarity. He inhaled the scent of her perfume. When she didn't resist him, he took it as a sign and pulled her even closer.

As their bodies pressed together, they moved in sync to the music. Song after song played as they continued to dance without words. Suddenly, the DJ cut in. "Okay, now ladies and gentlemen, lets slow this down just a little bit for all the couples that came out tonight. Men grab your ladies and ladies hold on tight to your man because we are about to get real sexy in here."

After the announcement, Erica disconnected herself from Kyle and began to make her way off the floor toward their both. Gently, he caught her hand and she turned around just as Freddie Jackson's "Rock Me Tonight" boomed out the speakers.

"For old times' sake?" he timidly asked. She paused briefly before replying, "I don't care about old time's sake. But for the sake of this moment, I will."

She pressed her body into his and dropped her arms around his neck. He looked down into her eyes and easily recognized the lust they betrayed.

She let her head rest against his muscular chest. She closed her eyes and hoped that he didn't feel the shiver that shot through her body. "I missed you, Erica," he whispered in her ear. "If this is only for a moment, then I never want this moment to end."

She heard the deep hunger for her in his voice. He pulled her even closer, grinding his pelvis into hers. She began to become aroused, feeling his manhood pressed firmly into her. He dropped his hands from her waist, resting them softly on her ass. The feeling of his strong arms holding her intensified the tingling she began to feel in between her legs.

"I need you, Erica. I've always needed you," Kyle continued to whisper in her ear. His baritone voice sounded so good in her ears along with the music.

"I need you back, Erica," he pled. She began to feel her heart rate increase and began to feel those old feelings arise. Those were feelings she was afraid of. He was beginning to do something to her. She could hear the desire in his voice.

It was coming from the depths of his soul. Two songs later, he was still grinding closely into her and whispering in her ear. She couldn't seem to control herself any longer.

"I want to leave, Kyle. Come on, take me with you."

Kyle hesitated a second, caught slightly off guard. He looked into her eyes and saw burning desire.

"Come on, take me with you before I change my mind," Erica slurred, seductively. He grabbed hold of her hand and led her away from the club.

Chapter Eleven

The ride back to Kyle's condo was one without words. Erica sat in the passenger side of his Hell Cat and tried not to think about the implications of what she was doing. Kyle pressed his foot down on the gas pedal, pushing the Hell Cat into overdrive. It had been some time since he entertained a woman and that had him feeling eager to get her home.

They pulled up to his condo and he killed the ignition. He got out and made his way around to open the door for her. Drunkenly, they both stumbled to his door he inserted his key into the door and let them both in. Before they crossed the threshold, Erica was already gliding her hand down the back of Kyle's head, softly touching the back of his neck. She sent shivers through his body with her gentle touch.

As soon as the door closed, he forced her body back against the wall. He began to kiss her with so much force, it was reciprocated by her, it felt as if they would devour one another. He grabbed her ass, she moaned softly and grabbed for his zipper to release him from his confines.

"Slow down, we have all night babe," Kyle said, before lifting her up and carrying her into his bedroom. He laid, her down on his king-sized bed and took a moment to savor her presence in his domain. "It's not too late for you to change your mind, you know," Kyle told her with no conviction in his voice whatsoever. In response, she lifted her arms and began to remove her dress in a striptease. Kyle climbed into bed with her and positioned himself between her legs. He began kissing her again, removing his clothes as he went. Soon, Kyle was completely naked as well he hovered over her, looking at the soft folds of her body. Erica began reaching for his length, she was dying for him to enter her.

"Tell me you want it," he teased her.

"I want it Kyle."

Kyle grabbed his manhood and began rubbing himself on the outside of Erica's pussy.

"How bad do you want it?" Kyle asked as he continued to tease her.

"I want it bad, please put it in Kyle. Please!" she begged him. Without saying anything more Kyle entered her slowly.

"Ahhh Yeah!" she softly moaned, as she felt him slide deep inside her. She wrapped her legs around his waist not wanting to let him go.

"Damn, you feel good," Kyle moaned into her ear. He had waited three years for this feeling again. Man was she hot, wet, and tight. He began to slowly stroke in and out of her. He pulled himself all the way out and slowly slid back in. He felt the searing pain of Erica's nails digging into his back in a passion-filled frenzy.

"Ohhh, yes, yes Kyle, you're going to make me come," she cooed, enjoying his deep thrust. Kyle began to increase his pace, stroking her with the right rhythm as her body began to shake. Slowly, everything inside her began releasing as she came with extreme force.

"I'm coming, I'm coming, oh my God! I'm coming Kyle!" She held on to him tight trying to allow the orgasm to run its course through her body.

Kyle lifted himself from her and commanded, "On your hands and knees now." It was at that moment she remembered the difference between him and Arnold. When it came to making love, Kyle took complete control of her and exerted his dominance and to her, there wasn't anything sexier. After she obeyed him, Kyle positioned himself behind her and allowed his hands-free reign over her body; he grabbed her rounded ass and thrust himself inside of her again.

Again, his thrust caused Erica to cry out his name. He felt completely in control and he wanted her to feel all the years of frustration he held inside from not having her. His pace quickened as the sounds of their bodies slapping against one-another filled the room.

She moaned softly as she looked back and began bouncing back, meeting Kyle's thrust.

"Tell me you've missed me," Kyle demanded while filling Erica up, hitting places inside her that hadn't been hit in three years.

"I've....missed you...ahhh...yes, I've missed you," Erica moaned in response.

Kyle could feel himself on the verge of exploding. He began to pull Erica back into him faster, trying to go deeper inside her. He closed his eyes and cherished the feeling of being inside of her. He grinded into her slowly and deeply once more before orgasming.

"I love you Erica" Kyle relayed. He was exhausted and out of breath.

I love you too, Kyle" Erica cooed before drifting off to sleep.

*****

Part Two

Love is a confusing and complicated emotion. It lacks the ability to be controlled. It has no restrictions whatsoever. Love has no limits on how long it will last, it has no limits in potency. Love will not shelter, and it refuses to choose who it will protect. Love will harm the innocent, will make confident the foolish and lead astray the most worthy. Even when we have thought to have mastered its mysteries, it seems to have its way of confusing us all over again. Why do we continue to seek out such a hurtful state of mind? Leaving heartache in our path every step of the way. I find myself wondering is there such a thing as love without fault? Or are we left here to mishandle one of life's greatest blessings...True Love.

-Erica Caldwell

I know you are probably wondering how a woman could who has been given so much from her man betray him so easily, the way I have with Arnold. I know because I myself wonder the same thing. The conclusion I have come to is that you cannot help the way you feel or who you feel it for. Love is funny that way, it's "supposed" to go this way or that way. But this way or that way might be the right way for you but who is to say it's the right way for me?

I bet you are saying to yourself that I'm wrong. You have probably pre-judged me as a deceiver, manipulator, and a cheater. Who is to say your judgement is correct? Who is better to say what's best for me than me?

I have compared the two men Arnold and Kyle. One of these men hurt me more than anyone else ever has and more than likely, ever will. What I want to tell you is that there is far more to that man than one lapse in judgement.

Together, we had been through so much. We learned about the wonders of love together. We figured out how to understand one another, how to properly please one another and how to properly push one another to pursue our goals.

Nineteen years I spent with him. So, I might ask you, was one mistake worthy of me throwing nineteen years of wonderful experiences out the window? When in reality, the good during those years far outweighed the bad. Should I have forgotten it all and not allowed love to have mercy on him?

Then there's Arnold who hasn't faltered or wavered in his love for me since the day we first met. The man that was patient with me when I did everything imaginable to run him off. A man that showed me love without flaw or doubt. The man who has been supportive of me and has pushed me to greater distances.

This is the man whose ring now graced my finger. A man who feels like he could spend the rest of his life happily with only me. A man who I must admit I've at one point felt similar for.

Now, I'm at a point where I really don't know what I feel. What I do know is that at this moment I want what I want.

Before you begin to judge me, please continue to read along and determine for yourself whether I'm right or wrong when it comes to this unforgiving game of love...

*****

Erica stood up and made her way to open the two-toned blue curtains in the master bedroom. The sunlight filled the room, but it did not brighten her mood. She would miss work yet again today and Debra would have to run the group as she had done for the last five days. Arnold had left an assortment of medications on her nightstand and refilled their mini fridge with plenty of orange juice and water. He hoped to help rid her of whatever virus or bug it was that she had contracted.

What he didn't know was that it was the love bug...

She walked over to the mirror and began to examine herself. Boy, did she look rough and unkempt. She felt that way as well. What should she do now? Kyle had made it known that he would do whatever necessary to have her, but he wasn't the only man competing for her heart. Arnold was her fiancée and he took pride in protecting the important things in his life. She knew he wouldn't accept someone threatening what he saw as his possessions. "What a mess," she thought.

She picked up the picture she took with Arnold on the beaches of Cancun, Mexico. The smile that he had on his face was priceless. That same thrill and excitement also showed on her face. He was happy and so was she as hard as it was to admit.

She looked at herself once again, staring long and hard as if she could see part of herself that she never knew existed. She ruffled her fingers through her hair and looked down before looking up once more. She had to make a decision one way or the other. Was what she had worth losing?

*****

Arnold sat at the desk in his study reading the newspaper. The news was the usual collection of madness and depressing events that transpired countrywide daily. The chaos that enveloped the world never seemed to desist, he closed the paper, disgusted.

He sat there reflecting on his own personal life. Things were seemingly picture perfect. His career was taking off as it never had before and as far as leisure went, he had ample time to enjoy himself doing whatever struck his fancy. There was only one thing in his life that was troubling him at this moment and that one thing was the most important thing in his world, Erica.

As he pondered the events of the past week, particularly Erica's purported "illness" something just wasn't adding up. He thought back to the week proceeding his business trip and the strange call he had received from Erica and her questioning him about the flowers that had arrived at her office. At the time, it seemed inconsequential but given her behavior the past week he had no choice but to ask the question: Was there someone else? Was she running around behind his back? He had never even so much as thought about her being unfaithful before. As things stood now, she hadn't left the house for days. Physically, she didn't seem ill one bit and when given the option of having a doctor come to the house she adamantly refused.

She had become distant, barely confiding in him. Ever since her birthday she had begun to act differently. He thought back to that day and how he had tried everything to make her smile to no avail. It was as if her mind was in a different place.

He took pride in his skills of observation; it was part and parcel of his success in business. His father had instilled it in him early on in life. He knew that something wasn't right and had made it his business to figure it out. He flipped open his MacBook Pro and opened Google and immediately typed in the name Kyle Malone. Pages filled with information and he began reading. The information took him all the way back to Kyle's days in college, he noticed that Kyle was an exceptional student and had graduated Magna Cum Laude with Latin honors. He continued to scroll and began reading up on the major acquisition of the World National Bank. He looked at the terms of the contract.

"A multi-millionaire, huh?" He said to himself and continued to read. He scrolled down and something that surfaced really caught his attention. The county clerk for Minneapolis stated that Kyle had recently purchased a condo in the area. Arnold's body instantly stiffened, he stopped reading and his mind began to race. The revelation had come to him. He instantly knew the answer to the questions he had posed to himself. He checked the date of purchase and noticed that it was around the time the flowers were sent to Erica's office. Everything made sense. He had been ousted by her old flame. He sat back in his chair panic stricken. His mind began to race, he wondered how far had things gone between them as of now? He began pacing the floor and he felt his face flush with anger. There was zero possibility that Erica didn't at the very least know Kyle was living right around the corner from them.

At that moment, Erica walked into his study, "Don't think too hard over there babe, or you will end up giving yourself a headache." She crossed the room toward him to see what he was doing.

"I won't" he replied looking up. Once he saw Erica, the look in his eyes changed from anger to affection. She walked up and put her body into his. She had a vulnerable look in her eyes which had the immediate effect of him wanting to take care of her.

"I see you are feeling better?" he said with sincerity.

"Yeah, I couldn't keep laying around like a sick dog forever. Besides, I was starting to look the part" Erica replied in disgust.

"I didn't want to be the one that said it but whew!" he joked. Erica chuckled too.

"So, what was it that you were thinking so hard about?" she asked.

"I was thinking about how hectic my schedule is. I have this meeting in Chicago tomorrow. Then immediately after, I have to fly to California for a weeklong convention. It's like I don't have any time lately," he complained.

"Your ambitions will take you to great heights Mr. Don't you ever forget that," said Erica reassuringly.

"I know," he replied. He wrapped her tight in his arms and kissed the top of her forehead as he stared off into the distance. He pulled away from her and began looking at her intensely in the eyes.

"What?" she asked regarding his uncomfortable stare.

"Just glad to see you are feeling better," he lied. He pulled her close again. "When you are down, I'm down. When you are up, so am I. I don't know what's been bothering you but whatever it is, never give it that much power over you because once you do, you give it power over me as well," he advised.

"I know baby."

"I'm glad you are feeling better," said Arnold as he released her from his hold and slapped her on the ass as she made her way out of his study. As soon as she left, Arnold picked up his office phone and set up a meeting that was long overdue.

*****

Standing out front of Swiss Account, Arnold admired the edifice. It was a sixty-story glass and steel tower, a nod to American architectural ingenuity. Inside, he paused briefly to check the directory that was attached to the wall closest to him.

"Accounting department, fifty-seventh floor," he read before making his way toward the elevator. He patiently awaited its arrival and tried taking the time to calm his nerves. He had come here to try gaining in understanding and had hopes that the conversation wouldn't spiral out of control. His father's words kept replaying in a loop in his mind, "Practice diplomacy until you no longer can" and that's what he fully intended to do.

The sound of the elevator opening broke him from his reverie as he stepped on.

Once on the fifty-seventh floor he exited. "Hello Sir, welcome to Swiss Accounts. How may I help you?" asked the receptionist.

"Hello, my name is Arnold Simmons and I have a twelve o'clock with Mr. Malone."

"Okay, if you could just give me a second, I'll phone up to him to inform him of your arrival. You can take a seat right over there while you wait."

"Thank you," replied Arnold who made his way over to take a seat. He picked up a copy of Black Enterprise magazine that sat on the coffee table. He began skimming through it and within ten minutes he was being summoned by the receptionist to follow her to Kyle's office.

"Mr. Malone, your twelve o'clock has arrived."

"Thank you Susan," replied Kyle as she exited. Leaving the two men to their business.

Arnold had to admit that the office was nicely spaced and properly designed. It had a masculine and expensive feel to it. He looked from wall to wall noticing numerous amounts of awards, certifications, and plaques. Along one wall was a book shelve and Arnold could see that Kyle was an intellectual reading man by the titles of his books.

"Welcome to Swiss Accounts," greeted Kyle with his hand extended out to Arnold.

"Thank you for seeing me on such short notice," he firmly shook Kyle's hand.

 "You have a really impressive office here, I must say."

"Comes with the territory," Kyle replied. "Let's have a seat," he motioned toward two chairs positioned looking out the windows.

"Kyle sat and Arnold followed suit. Arnold glanced at the pictures Kyle had framed of a wholesome older looking woman on his desktop. Arnold assumed her to be his mother. He continued to glance around but couldn't see a picture of Kyle with a wife and kids anywhere.

"Now, let's see here," began Kyle. "Okay, Mr. Simmons, I've had the pleasure of briefly reviewing your accounts and from what I can see, you've done really well managing your funds and investments. With the information that is available to me, I'm kind of wondering what your intention is in wanting to switch accountants?"

"Actually, I am not looking to switch accountants, Mr. Malone."

A confused look came up on Kyle's face, "Now I'm a bit confused then as to what is the purpose of your visit today. I'm sure you understand the service I provide is..."

Arnold cut him off by saying, "Actually there's another issue I was hoping you could help me get figured out today."

"And what that might be Mr. Simmons?"

"Erica Caldwell," Arnold simply replied. Kyle looked across his desk and realized who this man was for the first time. Now, he understood what this meeting was really about. He had only caught a glimpse of Arnold up until this point.

"Oh..." Kyle nonchalantly replied, leaning back in his chair. He loosened his tie just a bit before continuing, "I think you came to the wrong place, Mr. Simmons. I'm not sure Erica is an issue that I can help you with."

Arnold caught the arrogance oozing from Kyle's voice and demeanor. Did he know something that he didn't?

"I believe I've come to the right place. But if you cannot help me, then maybe it's me that can offer you some advice."

"I'm listening..."

"I think it would be in your best interest, Mr. Malone, to stay clear of my woman."

Kyle offered a smirk that quickly turned into a laugh, his chair rocked from side-to side yet he never broke eye contact. "How do you know that I haven't been staying clear of her?" he arrogantly asked.

"Mr. Malone, maybe I just missed the joke or maybe my sense of humor isn't as open as yours but whatever the case maybe, I advise you not to take this as a joking matter because if you do, I'm sure you'll be the one hurting in the end."

Kyle was to his feet just as quick as Arnold could finish speaking. He slammed his palms down hard against the top of the desk. "You have a lot of foolish courage to be coming inside of my office, offering up meaningless threats. From the look of it you seemed to be a pretty intelligent man, so for your sake, I'm going to give you the opportunity to use some of that intelligence and walk out of here in the same condition you entered," finished Kyle, who was towering over Arnold, chest puffed out.

Now it was Arnold's turn to offer up a laugh. Standing up, he made no attempt to leave. "Mr. Malone, I know all about the gifts you used to try to buy my fiancée's heart. What you might not have known, but now do, finances aren't an obstacle for me. You are not the only one with an eight-figure net worth. Next time it would behoove you to keep all of those extravagant gifts for yourself." Arnold said coolly.

"Again, I'm not sure-"

Arnold cut him off before he could say another word. "If that's the angle you are taking, it's a pathetic one. You can plead ignorance all you want but this will be my final warning. For your sake Kyle, stay away from my fiancée or I will be forced to make you stay away:"

Kyle quickly made his way around his desk toward Arnold. He stopped within inches of him and they stood toe to-toe, chest-to-chest, man-to-man. The tension was palpable and neither man gave the other any quarter.

Finally, Kyle began to speak in a calm voice, "Mr. Simmons, again, I'm sorry that I can't be of more assistance to you but as you stated yourself, I have an extremely busy schedule to keep so thank you for stopping by. It's been a pleasure, you can see yourself out. I trust you remember where the exit is?"

Arnold didn't move toward the exit. He took his time adjusting his tie and sized Kyle up. As soon as their eyes connected, he gave a look that conveyed abject hatred and distrust. After a moment, he turned on his heel and walked out of Swiss Accounts.

Chapter Twelve

Erica walked through the house, letting rose pedals fall loosely from her hands onto the floor. Arnold was on his way from Chicago and had planned to stop by the house briefly before making his way to California for the week. Erica was planning to see him off with some wonderful sex. She wanted to make it up to him for the way she had been acting. She knew their relationship deserved better and today she had planned to make it right. After she finished spreading the rose pedals, she made herself a glass of wine and got comfortable in their bed. She had on a lingerie set that Arnold had recently purchased for her, she knew that it would arouse him.

She was finishing off her third glass of wine and beginning to feel horny when she heard their downstairs door open and then close. She repositioned herself on the bed into a more sexually revealing position and she dimmed the lights to set the mood. Seconds later, Arnold entered their room. He paused briefly, glancing at her before making his way over toward the closet. Erica was shocked by his failure to pay her attention.

"Uhm, huhm," she made a show of clearing her throat in order to gain his attention.

"Hey baby," Arnold said, lugging a suitcase from the closet and tossing it at the foot of the bed. He began placing items into the suitcase.

"Baby, you don't see me laying here? I have that lingerie set that you been wanting to see me in."

"Of course, I see you," Arnold replied nonchalantly.

He continued packing his bags as Erica made her way out of bed and over to him. She squeezed herself in between the small space between him and the dresser.

"Excuse me baby, but you are going to make me late. I have a flight to catch and I'm already running late."

"I know baby, but I was hoping we could make love before you hit the road."

"I'm sorry, but I don't have time right now. My flight leaves in a couple of hours and I still have to make a quick stop at the office."

"Don't you think we can enjoy ourselves a little bit before you leave? You are going to be gone for another week and it's been some time since we last made love."

"I'm sorry but I don't have time right now," Arnold finished. "I promise, when I get home, we will have all the time you want, and we can spend a week in bed." He continued pulling suitcases out of the closet looking for the right one.

"Is it me baby? Am I not sexy to you anymore? You don't like this lingerie??" she pleaded with him.

"Baby, it has nothing to do with you, you know how important this trip is, I can't be late, that's all " he lied. In reality, his meeting with Kyle in Chicago had solidified his suspicions. The arrogance, the smirk on his face, his unconvincing denial of the allegations were all the evidence he needed to know that Erica's old sweetheart had somehow come back into her life in a big way. If she could-be swept off her feet by Kyle's tacky suits and expensive flowers then so be it, he wanted nothing to do with her. She disgusted him.

"I'm sure I'm not the only one that's horny right now," she purred seductively. She began rubbing Arnold's back and shoulders. Letting her body press up against his. She slowly moved her hands down to his zipper, fumbling to get it open.

"God dammit Erica! Is sex the only thing ever on your mind. Can't you see that I'm in a rush and have more pressing matters to attend to than sex? Excuse me," Arnold pushed her hands off him.

Erica back peddled until she hit the wall. She was in shock. As he finished packing, he looked at her with contempt. He grabbed hold of his bags and headed out of the house.

As soon as she felt he was out of earshot she broke down in tears.

*****

Erica walked along the trail by the lake, enjoying its breeze. She was with her father who had come immediately after hearing the sadness in his daughter's voice on the phone. She said she wanted to spend some time with him and needed advice about, of all things, relationships. She didn't specify but when his daughter needed him, he came. No questions asked. "So, what was it that you wanted to discuss?" Mr. Caldwell asked his daughter. Erica didn't reply right away. She wanted the right words to come to her. She knew her father wouldn't judge her and that gave her confidence to confide in him. Finally, she answered,

"I need some unbiased advice on my personal life," she stated.

"What part of your personal life?" he asked.

"My love life."

Mr. Caldwell paused briefly before replying. As a father, he naturally always wanted what was best for her. He'd always been straight forward with his advice, "Okay," he began, "what has Arnold done?" he asked.

"I think the appropriate question should be 'What has Erica done?'"

Again, Mr. Caldwell thought before replying. He stuck his hands in his pockets and prepared to give her his undivided attention. "I'm listening, sweetie," he told her.

"I guess I'll start at the hardest part and that is that Kyle's been back in the picture," she said cautiously.

"What do you mean by 'back around'?"

"I mean, he's in town, he's been sending gifts, and I saw him on my birthday." She paused, intentionally omitting details that she was positive her father could surmise. "He wants an opportunity to right his wrongs," she explained.

"Did he explain to you the reasons behind his wrongs?"

"That's the thing, I haven't even given him the chance to and I'm not sure if I want to. It's been a tug—of—war in my mind since he came back. It's got me so confused right now," she said, sadly.

"What is your heart telling you baby?" he asked concerned.

"My heart tells me to trust and have faith in what I already have in my life." Mr. Caldwell gave his daughter a chance to really think about the last words that she spoke. They stopped walking and began leaning against the rail that was overlooking the lake. He took a moment to savor the view while reflecting on young love's struggles. He knew them firsthand, his relationship with Erica's mother wasn't always a perfect one. By any stretch of the imagination. He wanted to tell Erica about how, at one point, he'd been both Arnold and Kyle. Instead he asked her, "Are you saying that your heart is still with Kyle, but you are afraid of losing Arnold?"

She nodded hesitantly in agreement.

"In that case, there is no right or wrong answer. You have to do what is right for you. No one else can tell you the right way to feel or the right way to love. Only you know what will make you happy. All I can tell you is to not allow anyone to abuse or misuse your feelings."

"The other thing I want you to remember is that you can't have your cake and eat it too. There are other people's feelings at stake here, darling," he counseled.

Erica took this in and watched the birds soar dangerously close to the water before averting themselves out of their dive back into the heavens.

"What if I decide to forgive Kyle and it backfires?" she finally asked.

"Then that will have to be a decision you live with forever. Sweetie, don't live your life being afraid of the what ifs because what if you forgive him and it ends up making you the happiest woman alive?" Erica nodded her head in understanding. Mr. Caldwell continued, "So what about Arnold, do you really love?" he asked.

"Yes, I mean I think so," she briefly paused. The fact that she could doubt whether or not she actually loved Arnold caused her to choke up a little. She held back the tear that almost fell. She continued to speak, this time with more conviction, "Yes, yes I do love him Poppa."

"Are you in love with him?" he asked with interest.

"I believe so, I Just don't know how I could say that I'm in love with him, but I feel as though I'm in love with Kyle as well," she finished with a hint of confusion in her voice.

"That's because the heart has a mind of its own," Mr. Caldwell paused for a second to wrap his arms around his daughter. "I just want you to trust one thing for me baby and that is when the time comes, you will know who you are truly in love with. Until then, you just have to live your life, but be careful baby because love is a dangerous game, and all is fair in love and war," he warned.

*****

The beautiful beaches of Miami, Florida were filled with tourists enjoying the sun and riding the waves that roughly hit the piers. They had made it down to Miami the day before in Lou's private jet after Lou and Cante called and invited them on the trip. At first, Erica was hesitant to accept because she still wasn't sure exactly what she was getting herself involved in. She thought back to the advice her father had given her and its implications. Her communication with Arnold during her trip was scarce. He'd called and checked on her a few times, but the conversations had often seemed forced and rushed. She couldn't say if it was coming from her end or if Arnold was slowly putting distance between him and her. She knew that, eventually, she would have to make some tough decisions but for the time being, she just wanted to live in the moment.

Erica, Kyle, Lou, and Cante laid out on the beach chairs sipping a variety of drinks with umbrellas in them, laughing and joking about the strip club scene they had explored the previous night. Cante had felt the need to compete for Lou's attention over the strippers which eventually led to her getting escorted off the premises. She took it upon herself to give Lou his very own private striptease and turn the middle of the club into the VIP room.

"You should've seen your face when that bouncer told you that you had to leave," joked Erica. "From the way you protested I would've thought that you really worked there," she continued, laughing hysterically.

"What you really should have been doing was picking up all that money that they were throwing my way. I didn't mind getting bounced out of there, I just didn't appreciate not being able to take my tips with me!" she said, dead serious while she sunbathed with Lou in her two-piece Dolce and Gabana swimsuit, sipping a margarita.

"Don't trip sexy, I'll tip you plenty later when you give me a private show," joked Lou before wrapping his arms around her, pulling her closer to him. She let her hand slide into the waist band of his Polo swim trunks.

Erica turned away from their embarrassing companions and looked at Kyle before she placed a kiss on his lips.

"What was that for?" he asked.

"Just impulse," she replied.

"I love impulsiveness," he said before giving her a kiss of his own.

"Oh, will you two please stop it with all of that lovey-dovey, I'm not sure I can stand it any longer," Cante said while pretending to be disgusted.

"Girl, shut up," responded Erica.

"How about we go for a swim," said Lou while lightly pushing Cante body from his and standing to his feet.

"What are you doing, Lou?" complained Cante "I'm getting a nice tan right now, can we hit the water in a little bit?" she asked.

"Too bad, the king rules," replied Lou before grabbing hold of her and lifting her up he tossed her body over his shoulders before she could contest any further and started running with her through the sands on the beaches toward the water. Her screams for him to stop and put her down fell on deaf ears as he laughed to himself. She continued screaming and flailing her feet before he took them both for a nosedive into the ocean. Erica was laughing at Lou's playfulness before she felt Kyle's body lifting from the beach chair as well. Once he got to his feet, she saw a playful look in his eyes that caused her to tell him not to think about it.

"Don't think about what?" he smirked innocently before grabbing ahold of her and tossing her over his shoulder.

"Stooppp, I'm not trying to get my hair wet" she screamed while being lifted up.

"Too bad, the king rules this beach," he replied before taking off with her toward the ocean jumping in alongside Lou and Cante. Once they came up,' they stood in the middle of the ocean and stared into each other's eyes. "Why don't you ever stop playing around Kyle?" asked Erica, feigning annoyance.

"Because you like it."

"Actually, I don't like it. I just like you and I don't know why."

"Because I'm different," replied Kyle before kissing her passionately on the lips.

"I'd hate to change the subject right now, but I'm curious to know, how are you able to do what you are doing without him noticing?"

"What do you mean?"

"I mean we are here in Florida, planning to stay for several more nights and he's not remotely curious as to where his fiancée is?" Kyle asked patronizingly.

"He's in California on an important business trip. I'm sure he thinks that I'm somewhere around town."

"Well, he should keep closer tabs on the things he loves before he messes around and loses them."

Erica looked into Kyle's eyes but didn't respond. This was the first time he had mentioned him and that made the severity of the situation become clear to her. Eventually, the two of them would cross paths if she kept this up and she knew that the results would not be good once they did. What was she thinking when she got herself involved in this mess? This was totally out of character for her, but she couldn't seem to control herself. She had planned to ride the wave until it crashed, just like the surfers. "What are you two talking about?" asked Lou and Cante, in unison as they swam up on them.

"We were talking about which couple would prepare dinner tonight," lied Kyle.

"I was thinking Erica and I would allow you gentlemen to cook for us ladies tonight," stated Cante matter-of-factly.

"I suppose we can make that happen, do you two lovely ladies like grilled-cheese sandwiches?" Lou joked.

"We aren't about to eat no grilled-cheese sandwiches, Louis," replied Erica.

"Well, that's the best I have in my repertoire," replied Lou.

"How about this? Whichever couple makes it back to their beach chairs last is the couple that has to prepare the dinner?" offered Kyle, while taking small steps toward the beach.

"That sounds like a good idea to me," affirmed Lou who stealthily approached Erica from behind, lifting her up, and dumping her into the water giving himself and Cante the advantage.

"Cheaters!!!" screamed Erica from the water as she watched everyone else swimming toward the shore.

*****

"You out did yourself this time," said Cante to Erica while laying back with her feet in Lou's lap as he massaged them. She made a show of rubbing her stomach to show that she was full from the meal that Erica and Kyle were forced to cook. The foursome sat around in Lou's rented condo listening to music, relaxing, and talking.

Erica and Kyle cuddled up and the conversation eventually switched to love.

"So, Lou, how many times have you been in love in your life?" asked Cante.

"How many times have I been in love...." repeated Lou before replying, "if I were to count on one hand, I'd have to say none," finished Lou.

"So, you are telling me that you've never been in love before?" questioned Erica while looking disbelievingly at Cante.

"Let me think about it, oh yeah, I forgot about the time that I bought my first Mercedes-Benz, boy was I in love with that..."

"Louis," scolded Erica, "boy we are not talking about no car, we are talking about being in love with a woman."

"Oh, in that case, the answer remains the same. NEVER!"
"What about you Cante asked Kyle.

"Well, I can say that I've been in love one time," stated Cante.

"With who?" questioned Erica who couldn't remember her best friend ever being in love.

"You must have forgotten about Rodney," stated Cante.

"You are talking about the man you met Sophomore year in college? Girl that was just lust."

"Lust, love, isn't it all the same thing?" questioned Cante.

"No, dear, there's a difference. Love is pure while on the other hand lust is artificial," replied Kyle.

"So, how many times have you been in love Kyle?" asked Cante.

"One," he simply replied.

What about you, Erica?" asked Lou.

The room fell deathly silent as they waited for her response. She could feel Kyle's body tense just slightly as she shifted in his embrace. How many times had she been in love? That was the million-dollar question?

"Twice," she said finally before feeling Kyle pull her into him even closer.

"Is there a reason why you've never been in love before Louis? I mean, do you believe in love or not?" questioned Erica, shifting the attention away from her.

"I guess I've yet to find that person who is capable of making me fall in love with her. I haven't closed myself off to the idea entirely, it just hasn't found me. I can say that I believe in love because I have witnessed it personally between people that have been close to me as I grew up. I just haven't yet found it myself."

"What about you, Cante. Why haven't you ever been in love?" asked Lou.

"I think finding love is harder for me than it is for others. I've always been a free spirit and have always liked a variety. I feel like, why force something with one person when you can enjoy it with...several. I'm sorry, did that just make me sound like a hoe?"

"No, it just made you sound like me," Lou stated with some admiration in his voice.

"If love found you Cante, would you embrace it?" asked Kyle.

"Of course, I would, one can't control the heart as much as we would like to."

"Isn't that the truth?" agreed Erica.

"So, Kyle, would you still say that you are in love right now?" questioned Cante.

"'Cante!" Erica said while giving Cante her patented 'you are going too far' look.

"No, it's okay," said Kyle before continuing, "I don't believe true love ever ends. I believe it may stall at times and it may be difficult to maintain at others, but it never fails. So, to answer your question, yes, I'm still in love and believe I will forever be."

The room fell silent. It had been over three years since Erica and Kyle were a couple so to hear him say that he was still in love with her did something to her that she couldn't explain. Was she still in love with him or was she in love with Arnold? She couldn't answer either with any degree of certainty. Just then she heard her phone begin to ring, and once she noticed it was Arnold, she got up and excused herself. The conversation continued between the three of them and it switched several times before they noticed Erica return with a solemn look on her face.

"What's the matter with you?" asked Kyle, concerned.

"That was Arnold, he ended his trip earlier than expected and he will be back in town shortly. So, I have to make it home to welcome him," she finished before heading off into the room she shared with Kyle to begin packing.

"I guess I'll phone the pilot and tell him to get the jet ready at the airstrip," Lou said with a hint of disappointment in his voice. Kyle made his way off the couch and into the room with Erica. He closed the door and leaned back against it. He watched as she packed her things back inside her suitcase.

"You know I'm not feeling this, right?" he finally said.

"Please, Kyle, you knew I already had an obligation before this started, don't make it harder on me."

"You are right, but eventually you will have to make a decision because I won't accept you having to fun off all the time. I'm not about to keep sneaking around. I told you that I want you back and I mean it. So, make up your mind," finished Kyle before turning and walking out of the room.

Chapter Thirteen

Once Arnold had made it back from his trip to California, he had made it his business to try and fix things between him and Erica. During his trip, he thought about her often but had decided that they needed this time a part. The meeting he had with Kyle confirmed that something was going on.

During his trip, he reflected a lot on his relationship. He couldn't figure out how they went from perfect to rocky so quickly. But then again, a part of him felt like he had the problem figured out, that problem he was convinced was Kyle. He had determined to himself that he wouldn't allow Kyle to disrupt what they had built. He loved Erica and reasoned to himself that even if there were indiscretions, that he would be willing to move past it. To him, not having her would be worse than any revelation.

After meeting her at home that night, he flew her directly out to France for the second time. He wanted to get her away from everyone and everything so they could focus on each other. He had figured that since this was the place in which she first fell in love with him that maybe it could be the place that helped their love survive.

The days passed quickly, and they were now on their sixth and final day of the trip. Arnold wanted this last day to be perfect, so he reserved them a private tour of the Louvre, followed by a romantic dinner at Erica's favorite spot to dine at while in Paris.

They arrived at the Louvre and began their tour. Throughout the museum were sophisticated displays explaining and showing some of the world's greatest love stories. They walked hand-in-hand slowly behind the tour guide as he pointed out and explained several of the works. Some of the stories dated back to the Renaissance. Arnold held Erica's hand gently, occasionally watching her reaction to some of the stories, particularly the ones that involved deceit. Some of the struggles in those stories were overcome but some proved too great to overcome, he secretly wondered how their story would end.

"Excuse me," Arnold interrupted their guide. "This display right here," he pointed. "What is their story?" he asked with genuine curiosity, pointing at an elderly Asian couple.

"Oh," began the guide, "I'm glad you asked, this couple here are Chu Makayuri and his wife. The figureheads of the longest-ruling dynasty in Japan's history. Their story is one of love's greatest."

"Please, tell us about it," said Erica.

"Okay. Well, once there were two very powerful and greatly respected dynasties. Makayuri and Sakimoto were the names, these families ruled Japan together for centuries. Ju Sakimoto was a princess and the youngest member of the Sakimoto family. Chu Makayuri was the prince and the youngest member of the Makayuri family. Both had bright futures with guaranteed positions of prominence in Japanese history. The two families had planned the courtship between Ju and Chu since the beginning of their lives. When the time came, they began growing strong and powerful. At the same time, another strong and powerful family began to emerge. The rise of this family caused disruption and chaos throughout the lands. Leading this new family was a merciless, handsome prince by the name Jin Yakatori. Jin was not only handsome, powerful, and merciless, but he was a charmer as well. As time passed, some of that charm reached Ju. She had begun going outside their lands to secretly meet with this new, charming young prince. After a while, the affair began to spiral out of control and eventually, the families became aware of her treason. The revelations crushed the empires and crushed Chu greatly. The families abruptly disowned her and put her into exhale in faraway lands. Once she was gone, Chu felt as if a piece of him were missing. He wasn't the same ruler without her. He began to feud with the rest of his family and the other ruling elite. As time passed, he became fed up. He personally exhaled himself so that he could be reunited with his one true love. The act resulted in chaos throughout the entire country of Japan. Once he reached the lands far away, he frantically searched for his damsel. Eventually, they reunited and built an even stronger love. Together they became the Makayuri II Dynasty.

Eventually, they would overthrow the original families and completely annihilate the Yakatori dynasty in a decades-long war that ravaged much of Japan. The

Makayuri II dynasty became and is still, the longest-ruling and strongest dynasty in Japanese history."

Arnold and Erica stood in amazement and stared at the old couple. After a moment's silence Arnold asked the guide to leave he and Erica be. Once they were alone, Arnold spoke, "Why do you believe a woman like Ju would jeopardize everything she had for something that was so temporary?"

"I don't know," replied Erica. "Maybe she lost her way somewhere and forgot what she really had."

"Or maybe she never realized what she had," Arnold suggested. They both fell silent; Erica began to think of her current situation and actions. She knew firsthand what it was like to lose your way. She knew how it was to be confused and excited all at once. She looked at the picture of Ju and stared into her eyes intently. What she saw was a woman who heeded guidance and respected love. Sort of like herself. She then looked long and hard at Chu and saw a man that reminded her of the man standing right beside her. She took a moment to gather her thoughts and then spoke,

"Do you believe Ju deserved Chu's forgiveness?"

"I believe the only person that can determine that has made his decision," said Arnold, he paused and then pulled her into his embrace. "I believe that he recognized she had had a moment of weakness and he was able to understand that sometimes, people get caught up in the moment and forget about both the past and the future."

"Would you have forgiven Ju?" Erica asked with curiosity.

"Hopefully, I will never have to be in that position," he replied before beckoning the guide back over to where they were standing. Together, they continued their tour mostly in silence and deep in their own thoughts.

Later that evening

Arnold stood in front of the mirror that was attached to his dresser and he straightened the collar of his white dress shirt. In their hotel suite he prepared himself for the final meal of their trip. Tonight, he had plans on enjoying a romantic evening with his fiancée and hopefully he would hear the truth out of her mouth in regard to what has been going on with her and Kyle. He examined himself in the mirror, straightened his posture and reminded himself of what his father once said to him, "Be a gentleman... Always"

As soon as he finished getting dressed, he walked inside Erica's bathroom and was taken back at how beautiful she looked in her backless gown. The silky material fit as if it were her own skin. The dressed flowed perfectly over her curves. He began to get aroused but managed to curtail his urges as he walked up behind her. He took a second to pull out the diamond necklace that he had bought as a surprise. He extracted the piece from its velvet box and brought it slowly around the front of her, draping it ever so gently around her neck and onto her collar bone and finally clasping it together at the back. "Now you have something that matches your ring," he told her.

Erica looked down at the necklace in awe and brought her hand up to gently run her fingers over it. "It's gorgeous," she gasped. "But it must have cost a fortune, how did you afford it? "'I know you have a well-paying job, but this thing must have been well into six figures."

"Don't worry about the price, please. Money is not something you should ever worry about if we are going to be together for the rest of our lives."

"Oh really, since when?" she asked almost jokingly.

"Erica, I have never told you, but years ago when my Dad died, I was entrusted with an enormous sum of money. As soon as I turned eighteen, I was able to access it. It was set up like that so I wouldn't use the money on frivolous things. I didn't want to tell you because I wanted you to love me for me and I didn't want finances to be the reason I was in your life."

Astounded, all Erica could think of to say was, "Thank you, baby."

He wrapped his arms around her and planted a kiss on her cheek.

"Sweetheart, you are going to mess up my makeup before we get to the restaurant."

"I'm sorry, I couldn't resist" he said playfully.

"That's because I'm irresistible," Erica joked.

"Yes, you are, now hurry up Ms. irresistible before you make us miss our reservation."

*****

Erica stepped aside and allowed Arnold to pull open the door to the restaurant. Once inside, they were greeted by the hostess and led to their table.

After a while, the waitress came to take their orders.

"Good evening Mr. and Ms. Simmons. Are you ready to place your orders?"

"Yes. We are. We'll have the steak special, medium rare, and please add a side of barbeque shrimp to each order."

"Would that be all, or would you like to place orders for desert right now?" asked the waitress.

"No, that will be all for now," finished Arnold.

Once the waitress exited, he took some time before speaking. He stared across the table at Erica and allowed his words to materialize.

"The last few weeks my mind has been racing with worry for you. Now you know, I know you like the back of my hand, so I know that it has to be something major bothering you. Talk to me Erica, tell me what's been bothering you."

Erica sat quietly for a few moments. She knew that she was being foolish to think that he wouldn't notice, she thought about opening up and telling him everything that had transpired over the past few weeks. She wanted to confess about the gifts and seeing Kyle, but she opted against it, knowing that no good could come of it.

"Baby, I've been going through a lot at work, the responsibility is a bit more than I'd initially bargained for and its sort of stressful," complained Erica.

Her voice conveyed nothing but exhaustion and on her face was an exhausted look. Arnold stared at her intensely without speaking a word. The silence stood for only seconds but for Erica it was much longer.

"If there was more bothering you, you wouldn't keep it from me. Would you?"

Again, silence overtook the moment. She looked into Arnold's eyes and felt the pace of her heart speed up. She felt horrible knowing that she was keeping things from the man who shared his deepest and darkest secrets with her. She reached across the table and grabbed his hand. She knew that she wasn't being true to herself by hiding this from him, he deserved to know what she had been up to.

"Baby, there is a lot that I would like to talk to you about..." she began but was cut off by the young waitress arriving with their food. She set their plates in front of them and uncorked their champagne. She sat it in a bucket of ice and walked away leaving the two by themselves. Arnold reached over Erica to the bottle of champagne and poured them both a glass.

They sat and quietly ate, looking at each other as if they were strangers. Arnold's expression betrayed his thoughts, he had a stern look on his face and she knew what this meant. He was deep in thought and she wondered what his reaction would be to her creeping behind his back with her ex-boyfriend. Furthermore, what would he say if he knew that Kyle was in town? She knew how possessive he could be and how he was willing to go to the end of the Earth for his loved ones. This is the part about him she feared the most, someone could end up getting hurt behind this whole situation. She felt as if they were at a crossroads, it was now or never. Tell him and risk the violence that would almost certainly ensue or keep it a secret and continue this relationship with the ultimate deception eating at her every single day of their lives.

She watched as he grabbed ahold of the champagne and filled each of their flutes another time. His eyes became fixated on her again while he drained his glass. She kept her eyes on his and watched him fill it yet again. He polished off his third glass and they finished their food in silence.

"So, what were you saying...when you were talking about something being on your mind?" he asked with an expression of genuine curiosity on his face.

"I've been having a lot of anxiety behind the preparation for the wedding. I'm having a difficult time getting the island reserved and I refuse to have the wedding anywhere else. Also, the designer I want for my wedding gown isn't taking orders until after the new year. I offered to pay extra to get put ahead on the list, but I haven't had any success. It's just becoming extremely stressful and it's bringing me down," she lied.

Arnold continued to stare over at her. He seen that she had the saddest look on her face but that wasn't the only thing the look on her face conveyed. Through her sadness he detected deception. She was keeping something much deeper than some minor wedding inconveniences from him and he was well aware of it. He knew that what she was saying was a lie.

"Do you want me to call a couple of my contacts and get the island reserved and get you bumped up on the designer's list?" he asked.

"No, the wedding preparations are from my responsibility, so I don't want to burden you with it. If I can't handle it within the next month then I'll have you help me," replied Erica.

"Okay," said Arnold while refilling his glass again. He took one gulp and finished it off. He made up his mind that he would play dumb until she decided to come clean with him. No, he couldn't figure it all out, but he knew it was something. He grabbed ahold of her hands and brought them to his lips giving them a soft kiss before speaking again.

"I'll let you handle things but if it continues to cause you stress then we will have to seriously consider getting a wedding planner to handle everything. Also, I need you to understand that I hate to be kept in the dark, so if there is ever anything else going on regarding you, I need you to tell me." He said this and then gave Erica a look that sent chills down her spine.

Chapter Fourteen

The cue ball deflected perfectly off of the eight ball, sending it into the corner pocket. Lou stood his stick up and with a satisfied look, informed Kyle that it was his third game winning consecutively.

"Yeah, I know. Congrats, you win again," he replied sarcastically while puffing on his cigar. The pool hall was filled with smoke. Lou made his way around the tableland pulled a stool up right next to his friend.

"I've noticed that you have been a little off your square lately bro, what's going on?" Lou asked.

"Just trying to figure out exactly what I'm doing with Erica. It seems like things are getting more and more complicated for me. It's like, on one hand, I'm getting what I want, but on the other hand it isn't enough because I need it permanently," he complained.

"Yeah, I understand. You just have to have patience. Allow things to run their course. You can't really expect everything to happen overnight. Especially being that you probably haven't even gotten her trust back yet."

"I understand that, but I still don't know how I feel about having her one minute and then having to give her back every night and having that knowledge and carrying it with me every day."

"Speaking of which," Lou said, "Do you really think that he is going to just let his fiancée go like it's nothing?"

Kyle paused and took a minute before replying. He set his cigar on the ashtray and took a sip of his corona before saying, "You know, I never told you this, but he showed up at my office."

Lou contemplated this before asking, "When did this happen?"

"A few weeks back," Kyle answered.

"So, what happened?"

"Nothing, really. I believe he was there fishing, trying to see if there was something more going on between Erica and me. He mentioned the gift I had sent her and faxed over his financials to show how much money he had."

"That was it?"

"No, he told me to stay away from her. He said that if I didn't. take him seriously I would regret it."

"Uhhh, he sounds like he is serious bro," Lou said, unable to mask the concern in his voice.

"The look that he gave me was definitely a serious one. I believe he meant what he said. It's just that I have my mind made up and my heart is made up too. I need her back man, you don't understand, she is the only one for me. I'm willing to confront anything that comes with that. I'm willing to face it all," Kyle finished.

"Some things are worth fighting for," Lou reminded him. He looked down at his text messages, (Hey sexy, have some free time and was wondering if we could spend it together.) He grinned at this and replied (sure).

"What's with the smile?" Kyle asked.

"Cante, asking to spend time together."

"So, what are you going to do?"

"I'm going to spend it with her."

"So what game are you going to play with her. Are you going with the 'I be super busy call you when I have time' game?" Kyle questioned seriously.

"Naw, bro. I think I'm going to take a different approach with this one," he replied.

Kyle burst out into laughter. This had been the first time he genuinely laughed the entire night. He'd always known Lou to entertain several women at once, usually only allowing it to drag on a day or two. The "game" was his thing. He had mastered the art of promiscuity. To him, he would always be too young to settle down. So, Kyle couldn't help but to laugh when Lou mentioned taking a different approach.

"Come on Lou, knock it off, don't tell me that the legendary Lou has found 'the one.'" He continued laughing before saying, "That was a good one, bro. Thank you for getting me out of my slump."

"No, seriously I'm really feeling her. It's like dating a female-version of me."

"Okay, now that sounds kind of freaky."

"No, seriously. Big Momma had invited me over for dinner and I'm seriously contemplating bringing Cante along."

Kyle laughed again but immediately stopped when he realized that Lou was serious.

"Oh, you are really serious?" he asked Lou.

Lou nodded and took a sip from his beer.

"I'm going to try it out. The only thing is, I'm having some reservations. She's so much like me that what if this is the time I'm being serious and it's her that is playing me?" Lou asked earnestly before continuing, "I'm afraid of getting 'playa karma,'" he announced.

"Listen, you are turning this into a science. You can't go into a situation with the negative possibilities playing in your mind. You have to give it a fair chance and if you end up getting 'playa karma' then you will just have to respect the game that you play." Kyle briefly paused, allowing his words to sink in before continuing, "I just believe that you sometimes have to take risk, because some risks are-"

"Are worth the reward," Lou finished for him. They both tipped their beers back, taking long pulls from them.

"So, what is your next step with Erica?" Lou suddenly asked.

"Well, she gets back into town tonight and we have a date planned for tomorrow at the Palace. It's about time I clear the air with her and let her know everything that I've been feeling," Kyle finished.

"Good luck with that," Lou wished him before continuing, "just be careful bro because love can make people do some crazy things."

*****

The following night, Kyle stood on the edge of the platform at the Central Palace. He had his hands placed behind his back as he looked out at the stars. He was allowing his mind time to clear while waiting on Erica to arrive. He had a lot flowing through his mind and needed to figure it out. He felt that he was all over the place with Erica. She'd let him in but kept him out at the same time. He began to think about the time they had been sharing over the past few weeks. They had good times and the sex had been mesmerizing. However, she wasn't only having good times and good sex with him. Everything she was doing with him, she was doing again at home with her fiancé, and that was the operative word... fiancé. This is what really kept him in limbo.

Since the time they were young he had always had her to himself, he didn't have to share her with anyone else, to do so was out of the ordinary. He began to walk back toward the center of the Palace. He looked at his watch and checked the time before taking a seat at a lone table at the center of the room. He began to rehearse what he planned on saying to her. He wanted this to go off without a hitch. He was nervous and anxious at the same time. He wondered what her response would be to him asking her to be with him and him only. Was she ready to forgive him and move forward? That was the million-dollar question.

Erica arrived at the Central Palace and headed up to the platform. She had received a call from Kyle the previous day asking her to meet him there and to dress elegantly. She wore an open back, all-white Valentino dress with matching Valentino Heels. She walked through the halls, heels echoing off the marble flooring, until she pushed through the doors to her destination. She stepped onto the Palace's platform and took in the breathtaking view. It overlooked the entire city of Minneapolis. The stars shinned brightly and aligned in the sky perfectly.

She glanced at the platform and noticed Kyle for the first time. Standing tall in his Ferragamo suit. He started walking toward her, holding two flutes of champagne. "Thank you for coming," he said. He grabbed her hand and led her toward their table. The lone candle flickered over the white tablecloth and cast shadows on the walls.

"This is really nice," Erica said as she seated herself.

"Yeah, this view is nearly as beautiful as you."

"Thank you," Erica said as she blushed.

Kyle grabbed ahold of her hands and brought them to his lips. He noticed for the first time that she was wearing the bracelet he purchased her. He looked into her eyes and said, "that's a very nice bracelet."

"Thank you, it is an amazing piece," she replied lovingly.

"Our meal should be arriving shortly, but first, there are a few things that I have been wanting to say. The first is that I want you to know throughout our time we have spent together you have made me a very happy man. You have given me so many wonderful memories and life experiences. I've learned so much from you." He continued, "Erica, my past infidelity had nothing to do with you. My actions were strictly egotistical, selfish, and idiotic. There was nothing that you did wrong or could've done better." He paused, allowing his words to sink in. "I screwed up....I mean..." Kyle's emotions came to the surface and he felt vulnerable in that moment, "...I want you to know that it was the first and only time that I will ever betray you. That decision has haunted me for years. I need you to know that my remorse and shame are real, and I am beyond sorry for what I did to you." Kyle's remorse was undoubtedly authentic, and Erica could take one look at him and see it. She looked into his eyes and was silent. She saw the sincerity and compassion that were beyond them.

"Secondly," he began, "I want you to know that I'm still madly in love with you. I have been in love with you since the beginning and it hasn't dissipated one bit. I stand before you today to ask you tonight to once again be my woman." Just as Kyle finished speaking the waitress approached with a platter filled with food. Kyle stuck his hand up, indicating that he wanted the waitress to allow them a moment of privacy.

"It's okay Kyle, let's eat. We have all evening to finish this conversation."

After the waitress served them their meal, Erica and Kyle sat and ate in silence and enjoyed the music and the rest of the atmosphere. After finishing their meal, Erica stood and took Kyle by the hand and led him to the edge of the platform their booth sat upon. She backed her body into his and he wrapped his arms around her. "I can still remember when we were in college, it seems like just yesterday. You and Louis were the talk of the campus and every single woman wanted ya'll. I can remember my first time not trusting you. I thought that you were with another woman and I was calling your phone incessantly and wasn't getting an answer. I made it to your dorm room, against my better judgement, and frantically beat on your door. When you finally opened the door for me, I barged in and searched the room for another woman, to no avail."

She paused, shaking her head, "I can still feel that moment when you pulled me into your warm embrace and held me. You wiped away my tears and asked me what was going on. When I finally told you my suspicions you didn't get mad at me you just laughed and then said, 'Erica, you are the love of my life, you are the only woman I have ever wanted. I love you and I am in love with you. Do not ever worry about me betraying you with another woman because I would never hurt you.' I can still remember that moment so vividly." Erica paused and a small trickle ran down her right cheek. "I trust you more than I have ever trusted anyone, but you hurt me Kyle. Even to this day I dream at night about all the amazing times that you and I shared back in those days. I often wish that we could go back in time but we can't Kyle. I came to the conclusion that no one is even close to prefect, although at one point I really thought you were the exception to that rule. I still love you and a part of me still wants to be with you, but I am not ready to be with you right now. So much has happened in my life since you and me. I still need time to figure out exactly what I'm doing with myself and my relationship... what I am ready to do is to tell you that I forgive you," she finished as Kyle pulled her closer to him. They both stood overlooking the city for a while before either one of them spoke again.

"Forgiveness is good for now," Kyle finally whispered before leading Erica into the middle of the platform. He held her close as they began to dance the night away.

*****

The days turned to weeks and weeks to months. Erica's indiscretions began to become more and more frequent. She was creeping off with Kyle so much that at times she would wake up in bed and forget who it was that was sleeping next to her.

She had become careless in her actions and found herself hiding her secret less and less. She couldn't understand the hold that Kyle had on her. It was as if she were in a trance, hypnotized by his caress and she couldn't get enough of it. He pleasured her so well and cherished her as if it were their first date every time, they were together.

Yet, she was still so confused, and Kyle was continually applying pressure on her to leave Arnold for good. For whatever reason though, she just couldn't do it. She wasn't sure if it was the security of knowing that she could trust Arnold and that he had never been unfaithful to her or if it was simply the fact that she wasn't sure if she could trust Kyle again fully. Perhaps it was both. That was the irony of it all, what she valued in Arnold she herself lacked.

One thing she did understand was that the game she was playing was a dangerous one and that she wasn't going to continue to win at it. Her luck would eventually run its course. Part of her felt like Arnold somehow knew about what she had going on. He never said anything directly to her, but she could tell in his mannerisms and the hurt hidden in those eyes of his. The pain that showed was the pain of knowing someone you love is finding happiness elsewhere, and she knew that feeling all too well.

Chapter Fifteen

"Hello, Sir, welcome to Forever United charity. I'm Debra, the assistant director, how may I help you?" said Debra to the handsome man.

The man looked around the office before replying, "I'm new to this area and was directed here as a good place to do donations and charity," he responded.

"Yes sir, you have come to the right place, indeed. Here at Forever United we specialize in helping children that aren't as fortunate as you or I. Most of the time they do not have anyone else in their lives and they depend wholly on the kindness of others. We have a variety of options for our charity events we accept donations on all levels. If you could please follow me, I can show you a pamphlet with an overview of our services," finished Debra as she led the way across the room.

The rest of the staff at Forever United were busy going over the plans for their upcoming event. Once Debra and the gentleman made their way over to the events display, she retrieved a pamphlet and handed it to him.

"We stage our events right here in Minneapolis as well as countrywide. They range from pledge drives to small item donations so you not only can decide where you want to help but how you want to help."

"Okay, so I'll have the assistance of Forever United throughout the entire process, from start to finish?" he asked.

"Of course, sir," Erica replied as she entered the room. "I'll take it from here, Deb, thank you for your assistance. Would you mind helping out in the other room for a little while, please?" It was more of a command than a question.

Debra had a slightly confused look on her face but obliged. She wished the man good luck before making her way into the other room.

"What are you doing here Kyle?" Erica asked sternly.

"I was busy going over some possible charity drives that I would like to host and on the verge of making a major donation before you rudely interrupted Debra and me," he replied in a joking manner.

"You must really be trying to get me killed showing up here like this. Arnold could pop in at any moment and as soon as he sees you and I together he is going to absolutely flip," she said nervously.

"I'm so tired of hearing that name and carrying on with our relationship behind closed doors."

"Please, Kyle we cannot be having this conversation here," she said before grabbing hold of Kyle's hand and leading him away toward the door. Before they could get there Kyle pulled her inside the bathroom and shut the door behind them.

"What are you doing?" she asked mischievously.

Without words, he gently pushed her up against the door and forcefully slipped his tongue inside of her mouth. She gasped and the initial shock of the experience caused her to momentarily resist his advances, but the kiss began to feel so good that she found herself yielding and moaning softly into his mouth. He placed his hands on the sides of her face and applied more pressure with his kiss. She began to rub his shoulders and back, moving her hands up and down slowly.

Kyle allowed his hands to roam all over her body. He began unbuttoning her blouse, lifting her leg simultaneously and grinding firmly into her. She quickly heated up and feebly protested, "Kyle...hold on...please...what if someone comes in?"

In response, Kyle reached above her head and locked the latch to the door, stifling her complaints. "Ohhhh Kyle," she moaned. She began unbuckling his belt and unbuttoning his shirt. She no longer held reservations as her hormones raged. He quickly pulled down her skirt and she stepped out of it. Her nakedness felt strange in this forbidden place, but it was exciting all at the same time. He lifted her body up against the bathroom door and entered her all in one motion.

"Ohhhh," she cooed from the euphoria. He was deep inside of her and she gripped the sides of his face, she gripped his shoulders and whatever part of him she could hold on to. His strokes were in rhythm and filled her with pleasure.

"Goddamn you.... you feel so damned....gooood," Kyle moaned as the door began rocking simultaneously with their motion.

Erica's moans filled the bathroom and the halls outside. She lost control of herself. Nothing else mattered except for that moment and she felt the thrusts that Kyle put on her. He began to hasten his pace, she screamed.

"Tell me that you are mine," he demanded in between thrusts.

"I'm....I...I'm" her words caught in her throat in the midst of the pleasure.

"I said tell me you are mine," Kyle demanded again before increasing the pace yet again.

"Kyle I'm I'mm...."

"Tell me now Erica, tell me that you will forever be mine," he repeated as he grinded inside of her tight and wet fold.

"Yes! Yes! Kyle I'm yours," she screamed and began to come with the force of a storm.

"Ohhhh...fuuuuuckkk," moaned Kyle as he exploded inside of her.

KNOCK' KNOCK KNOCK

A voice, "Is everything okay in there?"

Kyle quickly let Erica down and she covered his mouth as if to quiet any sounds that he might make.

KNOCK KNOCK KNOCK it came again.

"Excuse me, I said is everything alright in there?" it repeated. "Yes, everything is fine" replied Erica, clearly embarrassed.

"Oh my god Kyle," Erica whispered to where only Kyle could hear. Kyle began to snicker at her embarrassment and began getting himself dressed. Once they were completely dressed, Kyle unlocked the door and they both exited. To their surprise, the stranger on the other side of the door was an astounded Debra. Kyle quickly maneuvered past her, making his exit.

Debra stood, unmoving, with an expression of mixed bewilderment and disbelief. She wasn't the smartest person in the world, but she knew what she just heard anywhere and she for sure saw her boss and a strange man who she thought her boss just met ten minutes ago leaving the scene of the crime. Her head quickly followed the gentleman who was hurriedly exiting the building. She then turned back to Erica and gave her a look of disapproval.

"I was coming to tell you that Arnold was on the line for you, but I guess I'll just tell him that I couldn't find you."

Erica was humiliated as she watched her receptionist walk back to her desk.

"Shit!" Erica said, once Debra was out of earshot.

*****

Arnold sat parked discreetly down the block from the home that he and Erica shared. He had even rented a car to conduct his surveillance. Supposedly, he was out of town on business. That is, as far as Erica was concerned, he was out of town on business. It had come to a point where he could no longer go on leading his life with his suspicions floating in the air. He had to know one way or the other. He had never been an insecure man; he had never had to worry about fidelity with a significant other, but the past few months had been hell. He felt that he had always given his women plenty to be satisfied with. He was a provider, guider, protector, and advisor. He had been all of those things and more to Erica and all of this lay at the center of his confusion. What could possibly make her want to cheat?

His thoughts made him reminisce on his father and mother's relationship. He could only vaguely remember it but what he did remember was exceptional. His father showered his mother with gifts, they took trips together and as a child he saw the world. He remembered the looks of endearment that his father had in his eyes when he looked at his mother. That was, until the arguments began. He remembered the strain in his father's voice when he asked his mother what more did he have to do to make her happy. Finally, he remembered his father sitting him down and telling him that his mother had left. He told him that he shouldn't expect her to return and that it wasn't his fault. The same looks of happiness that love had put on his father's face were replaced by looks of defeat and it was love, again, that put it there.

Now here he sat, parked, and ready to follow what was supposed to be his fiancée. It made him wonder about what he was doing and why? How could he have given everything, and it still wasn't enough? He was instantly snapped out of his thoughts as he saw Erica exit their house and hop inside of her SUV. He allowed her time to pull away before trailing at a comfortable distance.

*****

Erica lifted her Prada shades above her head and sped through the city streets. She leaned over to press play so that the car's stereo would fill her head instead of her thoughts. She sang along to Mary J. Blidge before she was interrupted by the ringing of her phone. She accepted the call, "Hello?"

"Hey girl, what you up to?" it was Cante.

"Nothing, on my way to a meeting."

"What meeting is that?" Cante asked suspiciously.

"To meet a man about a dog, dang girl, you nosey," she replied acidly.

"Okay then Ms. Secretive. I'm just asking because I'm bored and want to get some lunch."

"Sorry, but I can't be your date on this one girl," replied Erica before asking, "Why didn't you ask Louis? Or did he already have his two chances?"

"Actually, he is in Europe right now so I can't ask him and besides, I think he might be the one. He has potential to make it to date number three."

"Oh girl, please don't tell me that out of all your conquests, it's going to be Louis that you end up falling in love with."

"I'm not saying that I'm tripping, falling, or anything. I'm just saying that I really enjoy his company," she explained.

"Yup, that's how it usually starts."

"Okay, enough about myself and Louis," Cante interjected, "so when are you going to have some time for your homegirl, or has Kyle taken up all of your time?" she asked sarcastically.

"I always have time for you, don't make it like Kyle's the reason," said Erica angrily.

"He is," Cante was serious. "That is who you are going to meet right now."

"Girl, quite being so nosey, it's a bad look." Erica, unable to maintain her feigned anger broke out into laughter as did Cante. The moment was cut short as Erica quickly peered over her shoulder; she had a weird feeling that she was being followed.

"Hold on Cante Let me call you back," Erica quickly ended the call.

*****

"Damn," said Arnold to himself. He watched as Erica sped up and began driving erratically. He slowed down and allowed her some distance. He continued following but as he did so he began to feel an agonizing pain shoot through his chest. He noticed that the direction she was headed in was foreign to her, it was in the direction of another upscale neighborhood, the one in which he knew Kyle's condo was located.

He slowed down even more allowing her more distance. He watched as she quickly swerved into a drive through restaurant. He shook his head, realizing that the feeling in his heart had turned into an agonizing pain. He continued right on past the restaurant, there was no need in following her any longer. He knew his way just fine.

*****

Erica quickly turned into the drive-through restaurant and watched as the car she thought could have been following her passed by. She proceeded out of the restaurant's parking lot and quietly cursed herself for being paranoid. She looked down at her phone, it indicated that a text had come. It read [Can't wait till you get here].

She smiled to herself at the message. It amazed her how he could still be so affectionate after so many years of knowing one another. The thought turned her on and made her kick the car into gear to get to him.

*****

The night was getting late and Arnold decided to finally call it one. He pulled away from a curb about half a block from Kyle's condo. After watching Erica arrive earlier and enter Kyle's place, his suspicions were finally confirmed. As he pulled off, the fact that she was still inside caused him tremendous pain. He headed back toward their house, deep in thought. He felt like his world was falling apart, right before his eyes. He stalled at a red light and before he knew it, he found himself repeatedly beating his fist down into the steering wheel. He felt exhausted and defeated just like his father had. He then placed his head down on- the steering wheel. He began taking deep breaths in and out, slowly reigning himself in and regaining his composure. The light turned green just as he whispered, "I promise to not be the only one hurting at the end of this," and then pulled off into traffic.

2 Days Later

Erica slipped into the bathroom and out of the earshot of Arnold as her phone vibrated with Kyle's number. After closing the door, she finally answered.

"Where are you?" he asked once she was on the line.

"Where do you think I am?" she asked rhetorically.

"I need to see you."

"Kyle, I can't, as a matter of fact I'm not sure we should see each other again."

"I'm not trying to hear that Erica; I need to see you today!"

"Kyle, I can't, seriously. This has all been a huge mistake from day one. I think that we need to end this before it gets out of hand," she whispered into the phone.

"Erica, it's already out of hand, can't you see that? I'll meet you in front of your office in an hour." He ended the call before she could respond.

"Kyle, hello....KYLE!" Erica said frantically looking at her phone to see if the call was disconnected. She angrily tucked it into her pocket before she exited the bathroom. She was taken by surprise by Arnold standing directly outside the bathroom giving her a suspicious look.

"Who were you talking to?" he asked.

"Debra," she lied.

"And you had to take that call in the bathroom?"

"No, silly. I had to use the bathroom and my phone rang," she replied before slipping past him and grabbing her jacket and purse. "I have to run to the office now, I'll call you when the day wraps up." She hurriedly left the house, leaving Arnold at the door.

******

Erica pulled up to Nicklelet Ave and parked in front of Forever United. She looked around the block before exiting her car. Once she saw Kyle's car, she made her way over and jumped into the passenger's seat.

"Okay, I'm here. Now what?" she asked.

"Give me a kiss."

"Seriously?" she asked while looking around the block nervously.

"I mean, we can sit here all day if you want."

"Okay," said Erica as she leaned in and gave him a quick kiss that turned passionate. She felt her body getting hot as their lips locked. Finally, she pulled away from him and checked their surroundings again. "Okay, now let me out and I'll follow you home." She got out of his car and got back into her Lexus.

Kyle pulled his Lexus coupe inside his driveway. They exited and made their way inside. The lights in the condo were dim and the sound of R&B played through the speakers. Erica made her way over to the leather sectional sofa and made herself comfortable.

"So, what was so urgent that you had to see me now?" she asked.

"I just needed you here with me today," he answered.

Erica became quiet before leaning her head back and closing her eyes. She felt Kyle's presence once he sat next to her. He let his hands roam over her thighs and stared at her intensely. He was still amazed by her beauty, even after all of these years.

He admired her beauty and was grateful that this was the woman that held his heart. For years he spent long days and nights praying to have her with him again and now those prayers had been answered.

"Come here," he began to say while grabbing hold of her hand, "I want to do it right this time," he said before leading her toward his bedroom.

He opened the door to his lavish room and stepped aside. She saw a bed filled with red, pink, and white rose pedals all over it. The lighting in the room was dimmed and the golden reflections of many candles positioned in the shape of a heart were burning. They gave the room a flickering glow as the shadows danced on the wall. Kyle let go of her hand and proceeded to find the remote to the surround sound system.

Erica took a moment to absorb the glamorous scenery. The romantic gesture was one she was used to; Kyle pressed the button to the remote and allowed Avant and KEKE Wyatts' voices to fill the air. The song fit the mood perfectly and the melody of "My First Love" began making love to their ears. He made his way back over to her. He came within inches of her before stopping. He didn't make any attempts to touch her, to feel her, or to even kiss her. He just stared down into her eyes and savored her presence. What he felt right then was what true love was. Erica looked up, returning his gaze. She, too, didn't make any attempts to act on her impulse to touch him, make love to him, or kiss him. Instead, they both embraced the unique feeling of two hearts beating as one. Finally, they embraced and softly kissed one another. Erica closed her eyes and enjoyed the shiver that ran down her spine as he kissed her. He kissed her again, softly and tenderly sucking on her bottom lip, allowing his tongue to explore hers. His gentleness instantly turned into eagerness before he took her into his arms. He lifted her up and carefully carried her over to the bed. He lay her down on the rose pedals and then began to undress himself, putting on a show for her. He removed a single piece of clothing at a time so she could take all of him in. Erica looked up and admired his broad shoulders and his muscular chest and six pack. Finally, her eyes settled on his well-endowed manhood. She licked her lips at the sight and began to unconsciously unbutton her blouse.

"Allow me," Kyle whispered seductively.

Carefully, he began removing her clothes, piece by piece until she was completely nude alongside of him. Slowly, he climbed atop of her until they were face-to-face again. He began sucking her lips into his mouth and enjoyed the feel of her breasts against his chest and his length against her mound. The chemistry they had was undeniable and their passion could no longer be controlled as the kiss turned fierce. The heat between their bodies was a steaming heat as Kyle lifted her leg into the air. He grabbed ahold of his manhood and positioned himself right at her entrance. Before he penetrated her, he whispered sweetly in her ear, "This is how love is supposed to feel."

The feeling of him entering her made her feel like she was staring into the night sky with fireworks exploding in it.

She thought that she would instantly come. Patiently, Kyle let her body become adjusted to his size, he lay still deep inside of her. The glorious feeling of her warm and wet insides was a feeling that he could never get tired of. Slowly, he began rocking back and forth inside of her. He took his time so that she could feel every inch of him. He wanted to show her how it felt to be made love to by someone who truly adored her. "I love you...Erica," he softly whispered into her ear in between strokes. He had so much that he wanted to say to her while making love to her. He wanted her to know how much he regretted hurting her. He wanted to tell her about all the dreams he had been having of her over the years. He wanted her to know how incomplete his life had been since the day she walked out of it. He wanted to tell her that no woman had been able to compare to her since and that he needed her in the worst way. Instead of telling her he let her feel it through his loving touch, and he knew the effect was indeed greater.

Slowly, he started to pick up his pace, rocking in and out of her with perfect strokes. He looked into her eyes and seen passion seeping from them, he also seen pain seeping from them as well. Erica placed her hands on his buttocks and pushed him further inside of her. The feeling he was giving her was an amazing one. She gasped to keep the tears from flowing. He began to make love to her even faster while never breaking eye contact with her. The mixture of pleasure and pain was overwhelming and before she knew it, the tears had started to fall. Their souls were so connected that the same pain caused tears to also flow from his eyes as well. Nineteen years of experiences, conversations, trust, love, and finally, pain all seemed to be released at that moment. Words no longer needed to be conveyed to know that in those seconds forgiveness was found. The pleasure began to override the pain as both Kyle and Erica began to come together in an Earth-shattering orgasm. Slowly, Kyle collapsed on top of her. He carefully began to wipe the tears away from her face and she too did the same to him. They stared into each other's eyes and wrapped their arms around one another. The sounds of "My First Love" playing in the background sealed the mood.

"I love you, Kyle," Erica softly whispered into his ear.

Only another second passed before he responded with, "I love you too, Erica...a lot, a lot," and they both drifted off into a slumber.

Chapter Sixteen

Arnold stood inside the dimly lit living room with a bottle of whisky in his hand, slowly rocking and wobbling from side-to-side. Luther Vandross's "A House is Not A Home" was playing throughout the house. He tried gathering his balance before drunkenly stumbling toward the fireplace. Once there he leaned on it briefly before reaching and snatching up a picture framed of himself and Erica. Looking at it, he began to sing along to the music A chair is still a chair, even if there is no one sitting there, but Ohhhhh, a chair is not a house and house is not a home, when there's no one there to hold you tight....

Clumsily, he took another gulp of whiskey and felt a tear slide down his face. "How could all of this be happening?" he thought as another tear followed. Why hadn't she told him that she wasn't happy? How could they be living a lie when things seemed perfect? What about everything they had been through together, had she forgotten it all? He began to think about the first time that she had said she loved him. He'd thought that in that moment she'd surrendered her heart over to him. He'd thought wrong... His next thought of her accepting his marriage proposal broke him down to his knees. Holding his arms out to the sides, bottle dangling from his hand, he began to yell,

"WHAT MORE? HUH?....WHAT COULD YOU HAVE WANTED?"

Tears continued streaming down his face and he began to visualize her laying in Kyle's arms. How could she be betraying him with the one who had betrayed her? What kind of sick irony was this? Throughout their relationship he had been faithful and loyal to her. He had been everything he could be and given his all and yet, it wasn't enough. He slung the picture across the room continuing the sing along..."A room is a room, even if there's nothing there, but gloom, but ohhhh, a room is not a house and a house is not a home, when the two of us, is far apart and one of us has a broken heart..."

His thoughts went back to the day his mother had walked out on him and his father. He remembered that in the days to come his father never knew of him hearing him silently sob throughout the middle of the night as he called out for her. He could still remember when his father began to walk with his shoulders slumped and remembered the empty liquor bottles that began turning up at the bottom of the trash bags. He began to sob even harder from these memories. He tried taking another shot of whiskey but lost his balance, falling completely to the floor. He began laughing hysterically to himself, losing complete control of his emotions. Slowly, he picked himself off the floor. He struggled as he walked toward his armory containing his arsenal of weapons. Once there, he snatched it open and grabbed hold of his Colt .45 pistol. After pulling a box of .45 caliber shells from the shelf he began slowly loading the magazine, one bullet at a time.

He stumbled again toward the winding stairs and recklessly pointed the firearm in the air. He let off a round that went into the hanging chandelier. Hysterically, he began laughing again before dancing with himself along to the song...."Darling have a heart don't let no mistake keep us a part, I'm not meant to live alone, turn this house into a home, a home when I climb us there..."

After climbing the stairs, he made his way into their bedroom and to a chair that was sitting in the corner. He plopped down into it with his gun still in his hand. Leaning his head back, he closed his eyes and began patiently waiting for Erica to return home.

*****

She made her way into the entrance of their home, she was met by silence when she entered, she quietly stepped out of her heels and sat the bag at the side of the door. She began to tiptoe her way up the stairs, slowly discarding pieces of her clothing. She stopped at the top of the stairs in her tracks as she thought she heard sounds coming from their bedroom. She remained still in hopes that her surprise wouldn't be spoiled. When no one exited the room, she continued on with her mission. She stripped down to just her thong as she reached for the door handle and slowly began pushing open the door...

What she saw next confused her and hurt her all at once. For a second, she thought she might have entered the wrong house. There was a woman there in bed, riding slowly up and down on top of a man. The man gripped her tightly and moans of pleasure were being emitted from their mouths. She stood frozen, not knowing whether to announce her presence or turn and leave as if nothing had happened. Finally, she was able to speak but the only thing that came from her mouth was Kyle's name. Instantly, Kyle tossed the naked woman from on top of him and he tried covering himself as he watched Erica standing frozen in the doorway. The hurt in her eyes were evident as everything she thought she knew that she thought she admired and loved came crashing down before her eyes. Finally, the strength came to her legs and gave her the power to turn and run, ignoring the wails of Kyle's voice, repeating her name over and over again...

"Erica!! Erica!! wake up!" Kyle's voice sounded strained with worry as he woke her from her nightmare.

Erica jumped up from her sleep. She looked around disoriented while trying to figure out where she was at. She felt sweat dripping from her forehead as she struggled to free herself from Kyle. The contents of her dream suddenly came to her and she felt her heart flutter. The sight of the man of her dreams betraying her with another woman was just too much.

Kyle tried pulling her into him, but she fought with all her might to free herself...

"It's okay, Erica, you were just dreaming."

"Let go of me Kyle, please let go of me."

She felt like she was lying in the arms of the enemy.

"Calm down, Erica, you were having a nightmare."

Erica quickly broke free of him and made it to her feet. She began to scramble and find all of her belongings that were scattered around the room.

"What are you doing? Where are you going? It's 3 o'clock in the morning."

"I have to go; I just have to," Erica finished before grabbing ahold of her things and rushing out of the bedroom and out of the house.

*****

What was I thinking getting involved with him? Erica thought to herself as she rushed home. She pressed down harder on the gas pedal. She examined the clock, it read 3:30 a.m. She sent a silent prayer to whoever or whatever was above that Arnold would be fast asleep. How could I be out here deceiving the man that has been so good to me for a liar and a cheater? The irony in her actions were all of a sudden apparent for the first time. Her mind was racing as she quickly pulled into the driveway of their home and killed the lights. She hopped out and made her way into the house as quietly as she possibly could.

She removed her heels after walking through the front door. She allowed her eyes to adjust to the darkness and again prayed that Arnold was sleeping. She began to tiptoe her way through the house. She hid her overnight bag in the hall closet and then made her way up the stairs toward their bedroom.

The door to their bedroom was closed and no reflection of light could be seen under the door. This was surely a sign that Arnold was asleep, wasn't it? She slowly twisted the knob and began pushing the door open, she flinched at the creaking sound the door made. Again, she tried letting her eyes adjust to the darkness before moving anywhere. As soon as she started moving again the lights filled the room. "Oh, my! Arnold! You scared me! What are you doing??"

Arnold was sitting in the corner in the room. Erica asked him, "What were you doing sitting here in the dark? Are you okay?"

"I guess I should be asking you what are you doing creeping around in the darkness?"

"I wasn't creeping, I just didn't want to wake you up."

"Well, don't worry about me, I'm wide awake," replied Arnold. He allowed his eyes a moment to pierce right through her and she instantly looked at the ground, averting his gaze.

"How was work today, baby?" questioned Arnold suspiciously. "It must have been a very busy day given the fact that you are coming home at 3:30 a.m.," he said, glancing at his watch.

"Work was very demanding, even with Debra helping me most of the way," she lied.

"That's funny, because when I tried bringing you lunch today, Debra said that you took the day off."

"Oh, that's because I left to have lunch with mommy and daddy and then I finished my work at their house this afternoon."

"Interesting, because after I left Forever United, I swung by your parent's house and both of them said that they hadn't seen or heard from you the entire day." Arnold paused briefly before continuing, "So where have you really been, Erica?"

"I....uhhhh...well..." stuttered Erica as she watched Arnold lift from his chair and walk toward her. Seeing the gun in his right hand for the first time, she slowly backed away from him until her back hit the wall. As Arnold got closer, the look in his eyes made her heart begin to beat rapidly. She had never seen him with such a deranged look in his eyes.

He came within inches of her face and began speaking, "Three years I have known you Erica and I've never known you to be a liar. I've never known you to act the way you have been acting lately. The sneaking around, the missing my calls, stuttering when you speak. I've always been conscious of what surrounds me, and I've never neglected to notice a difference in my woman. So, did you really believe that I would remain ignorant?"

"Did I think you wouldn't notice what, exactly?" Erica asked, playing dumb. Just as she finished her statement, she felt a fierce wind whoosh past her. It was Arnold's fist crashing into the wall directly behind her head. A quick scream of surprise escaped her as shock took over.

"Don't you dare play me for a fool Erica. Don't sit here and disrespect my intelligence. I'm very aware, I know all about the gifts, I know about the trips, the meetings, and the late nights...I know all about Kyle."

Hearing Kyle's name come from Arnold's mouth made her weak in the knees. Tears began to stream down her face and her body involuntarily slipped to the floor. How much did he know? She wondered before pulling her knees to her chest as Arnold stood towering above her. Slowly, he began to crouch down, bringing himself face-to-face with her. He brought his lips close to her ear and began to whisper.

"I stood down for you when I had no reason to. I was patient with you. I was understanding to your pain, I was considerate to your indecisiveness and I put up with your mood changes. I've been nothing but loyal to you at a time that you couldn't find it elsewhere and this is how you repay me, huh? With the same man that broke your spirit to begin with?" He paused briefly, to let his words sink in.

Erica began sobbing uncontrollably as his words penetrated deep into her heart. She felt horrible knowing that she was breaking the heart of the very person who once helped her heal.

Arnold continued, "Congratulations, Erica. You've now become the very person in which you once despised. But I refuse to allow this to break my spirit. I refuse to allow him to come along and take everything that I've worked hard for away from me. I love you, Erica. I love you with all my heart. I need you to understand that I'm willing to die for what I love. So, I hope he is too," Arnold finished his tirade before getting back to his feet. He grabbed his keys and headed out the front door. Hearing Erica crying behind him and feeling his heart breaking all at once.

*****

Ding Dong...Ding Dong....

Kyle grudgingly made his way to his feet after hearing the doorbell sound off several times. He didn't have the strength or wasn't in a good mood for company after how his night ended with Erica. He just didn't understand why she had run from him. He hadn't done anything wrong from his recollection. He was so lost in the confusion of love that he just wanted to stay hidden forever. "Who is it?" he screamed once he made it to the door. He didn't get a response, so he repeated himself again before forcefully yanking the door open.

"I said, who is it?" he began to yell but stopped at the sight before him. Erica had her hair down, frazzled and face stained with tears while hugging herself tightly.

Seeing her standing there in such a vulnerable and pathetic state almost broke his heart. Without any words, he stepped into the hallway, wrapped his arms around her and brought her into his home. Once inside, Erica couldn't contain herself as a rush of tears flood from her eyes. Kyle continued to hold her close without speaking. After several minutes her sobs began to subside.

"Are you okay?" he finally asked. Erica shook her head in the negative and removed herself from his embrace. She stood before him without speaking and he allowed her the time needed to gather up her thoughts. After awhile, they both stopped staring at one another, finally she began to speak in a shaky voice.

"I can't do this anymore Kyle."

"You can't do what anymore?"

"This...whatever this is. The sneaking around, the lying, the cheating, this isn't me Kyle. This isn't something that I want to be a part of anymore."

"I understand what you are saying but you knew what we were getting ourselves involved in. You are only being sneaky because you want to be. A choice could easily be made, him or me."

"I don't want to choose between the two. I don't want to hurt anyone, or I don't want to get hurt myself. I just want things to go back to the way they were, I don't want to be confused anymore Kyle."

"Call him right now and tell him you are done with him and the confusion ends," Kyle said.

"Maybe it isn't him that I'm trying to be done with," Erica said, her words surprised Kyle more than a little. He took a step back while trying to allow her words to register. He had thought that over the past couple of months he had won her back. Now he didn't know what to think.

'So, what are you trying to say? I thought...."

CRASH!!!

Before Kyle could finish his sentence, the loud sound of the door crashing in took him by surprise. Instantly, he went to shield and protect Erica from whatever was happening. After securing her he looked toward the door, and what he got was a terrifying sight and it frightened him to his core.

Coming his way was Arnold with a deranged look in his eyes, wielding a large automatic pistol. Quickly, Arnold was in front of him and before he had time to react, he felt a stinging blow on his jaw. Arnold's left fist had hammered into him and it instantly dropped him. "Nooo!" Erica screamed. She placed her body between the two men. She sacrificed herself to prevent Kyle from receiving any further abuse.

"Arnold, please do not do this!" she pleaded.

"Move out of the way, Erica! You cannot protect him now." Arnold had the look of utter insanity on his face as he said this.

Kyle was dazed and couldn't make sense of what was being said. The room seemed to be spinning and as he tried to stand back up, he fell immediately to the ground.

"Please, Arnold, I came here to tell him that I am ending it. I don't want him or this. All I want is you Arnold. Please, put the gun down baby. Let's leave and we can work on us."

"It's too late for him. I warned him to stay away and he refused to listen. Now he must pay for his disrespect of what you and I had."

Kyle stumbled to his feet while regaining consciousness. His vision became clearer and the words between Erica and Arnold became crisper. Hearing Erica pleading for his safety gave him the strength to get back on his feet. He wiped the blood that was trickling from the sides of his mouth with the back of his hand.

"Now you are being a man," began Arnold, "stand on your own two feet and face me like a man. I told you that you would regret it if you continued to pursue my woman. Now, do you understand that I wasn't joking?" Arnold asked, tightly gripping the pistol that he held in Kyle's direction.

"Do you think your warning was supposed to deter me? I'm a man that goes after what he wants regardless of the consequences. So, go ahead, shoot me if you are going to because I will not stop until I get her back."

Kyle watched as Arnold gently moved Erica from between them. He placed her behind him while still pointing the gun at Kyle.

"Please, Arnold, let's just leave," Erica begged him before directing her attention to Kyle. "Kyle, what we had is over with. I don't want any part of it any longer. All I want is to make things work with Arnold. I'm sorry to have led you on but what we had was part of my past and that's where I want to leave it," she finished.

"That's the choice you want to make Erica? Him over me?" asked Kyle with agony in his voice.

"You heard her correctly," responded Arnold before continuing, "but look at the bright side of it, you might not get to leave with the woman but at least you get to leave with your life still intact" he finished with an arrogant chuckle.

Before Kyle knew it, he found himself lunging at Arnold. He grabbed hold of Arnold's arm and the gun and a struggle ensued. Kyle used all of his strength to slam Arnold into the wall.

He held Arnold's hand high directing the pistol toward the sky. Arnold quickly brought his knee up and slammed it into Kyle's midsection, next he head-butted Kyle causing him to temporarily lose grip on Arnold's arm.

The head-butt discombobulated Kyle as he lunged blindly and wildly in Arnold's direction again...

BOCK!!!!....

The deafening sound of the pistol, firing echoed off the walls of the condo. The sound was piercing, and time seemed to stand still at the moment. Erica watched as the smoke slowly simmered from the barrel of the pistol. She felt the screams that escaped her mouth but couldn't hear a sound as she watched Kyle's body slump to the ground with blood streaming out.

Part Three

We travel this world blindly in love trying to figure out the right way to go. Along our journey we explore different paths, paths of enjoyment, satisfaction and fulfillment. We also explore different roads, roads of confusion, doubt and lust. In love there lies a mystery, a mystery that has the power to take the soul along a soaring high or that can break the heart a million ways than one. Love is an emotion which is controlled by human's natural flaw. Every time you explore it with someone differently you have the possibility of experiencing a different result. Love is a feeling that could be so great that it overwhelms you, it can also be so out of control that it breaks you down badly. I stand here unshaken and unafraid of this mystery they call love. And I want you to take this chance on love with so that we can see that love is one beautifully flawed emotion that is meant for you and me!

- Arnold

The deafening sound of the pistol firing echoed off the walls of the condo and time seemed to stand still that very moment. Smoke simmering from the barrel of the pistol was all that could be seen by Erica's her vision became tunnel. She stood in shock, glancing from Arnold whose hand was now shaking uncontrollably while still gripping the pistol, over to Kyle whose body slowly slumped down the wall of the condo leaving a trail of thick blood against it. She tried screaming but no sound came from within her. She tried taking steps toward Kyle in order to aide him, but her feet felt like cement blocks that was stuck to the ground below.

"Arnold!!! What have you done?" Erica questionably screamed once her words finally materialized. Finally, she gained control of her movements and proceeded toward Kyle's side.

"Kyle!" she screamed while bending down to his aid. "Kyle!! Kyle!! Please be okay Kyle!!" She placed her hand against his wound in efforts to stop the steady flow of blood that leaked out. She tried lifting his head which leaned helplessly to the side.

"Kyle please get up," she stated before reaching for his wrist to check him for a pulse and sign of life.

Arnold stood behind her in shock as the gun slipped from his hand onto the solid marble flooring below. "What have I done," he thought to himself as a tear escaped his eye. The realization and seriousness of what he'd just done became apparent to him and it panicked him. He wanted to get his point across to Kyle about leaving his fiancée alone, but never imagined that things would really spiral this far out of control. He looked from Kyle to Erica, then back to Kyle once more. Kyle's body looked lifeless as blood seeped continuously from his wound. He then tried taking steps toward Kyle in order to help aide him but was cast in the same trance that Erica was only minutes before. He was trying to grasp the situation that had unfolded before him but wasn't able to. Even though he didn't have intentions of actually harming Kyle, standing there seeing Erica at Kyle's aide and showing her concern and love for him made his action feel less regrettable. At that moment he wanted so badly to go over and pull her from Kyle's side so that Kyle could feel the wrath of the pain caused by creeping with another man's woman.

Suddenly a shacky voice announced, "I'm okay...I'm...I'm okay." The words seemed to pierce through both Arnold and Erica's ears as Kyle showed life. A sense of relief swept through both their bodies.

"Oh my god!! You're okay! You're okay repeated Erica as she cried tears of joy for the life that Kyle showed.

Kyle managed to reach for the wound that opened his shoulder. He grimaced from the pain of contact and his hand became soaked instantly from his own blood. He fought off the shock that tried to ensue due to seeing so much blood.

"I need an ambulance," he mustered up the strength to announce. "Of course!! Of course, you do!!" replied Erica urgently, "I'll call them now!" she finished before hurrying for her purse that held her iPhone.

"NO!!" said Kyle, stopping Erica in her tracks. "NO!!" he repeated before continuing "If you call them now...someone is going to jail." He paused briefly trying to gain his strength because he felt himself losing consciousness and control. "Both of you just leave. I'll call and and I'll say that I had an intruder that I fought off"

"No Kyle, I cannot leave you in this condition. What if..." Erica was interrupted again by Kyle.

"Just leave, I'll be fine. I brought this upon myself so I must handle it by myself," he finished weakly.

"But..." Erica tried contesting again before Kyle cut her off once again.

"No buts," said Kyle weakly before continuing. "Just hurry and get out of here." He grabbed his phone from his pocket and dialed 911. He watched Erica quickly run to Arnold's side. His vision became blurry before he observed Arnold bend down to retrieve his firearm. "911 dispatch, what is your emergency?" Asked the dispatcher on the other end of the phone.

"I've...I've had an intruder at 6100 north plaza..." began Kyle, "And I've been shot," he finished. His vision and understanding became distorted and right before he slipped from consciousness the last thing he seen was Arnold and Erica quickly rushing out of the condo.

7 months later...

"And Erica do you take this man to be your lawfully wedded husband? For better or worse? To have and to hold? Through sickness and health?" asked the preacher as he stood before the center of the alter.

Erica stood tall in her see-through veil that covered her face staring into Arnold's eyes after he just said yes and contemplated the preacher's words. Would she hold true to and honor her vows through sickness and health and better or worse? She quickly began to reflect on everything that they'd been through over the years. She thought back on how Arnold had won over her heart after she'd run from Kyle. Next, she thought back on her deception of Arnold and how it led up to Kyle being shot. Finally, she thought about all of the counseling sessions that her and Arnold endured in order to get their relationship back on solid ground. Now, as she stood at the alter looking Arnold in the eyes, she had to admit for him she would hold true to those vows just the way he'd held true to her.

"I do!" she finally said as a tear stained her mascara. "Okay, then by the powers invested into by the courts and by god, I hereby pronounce you husband and wife. "You may now kiss the bride."

Arnold leaned over and Erica reached up to wrap her hands around his neck as their lips locked in a passionate kiss that sealed their union. Slowly they detached and Arnold looked down into Erica's eyes before speaking,

"I love you so much, Mrs. Simmons." "I love you even more Mr. Simmons," Erica softly replied. Arnold took Erica's hand and guided her through the sands of the Belize beach front resort. The attendees all began to assemble and follow the couple to the makeshift dance floor and after Erica threw her flowers into the crowd of eager women wishing to one day be married as well, everyone began to dance. Arnold pulled Erica's body closely into his, allowing her to feel his warmth as well as his heartbeat. He held her tightly and she held him similarly. As they danced, Mr. and Mrs. Caldwell made their way beside them. Erica glanced over at her mother and father and smiled. They were the epitome of what she wanted for herself and Arnold, a long lasting, union of real love, dedication, and prosperity. 40 years wasn't an easy task to achieve but they'd accomplish it and now Erica intended to have the same results with Arnold. Erica and Arnold danced for several more songs before Arnold whispered into Erica's ear that it was time for them to sneak away. They snuck away leaving the guest to continue to enjoy the festivities. Once they made it inside their limo, Arnold pulled Erica's body into his and kissed the top of her forehead.

"You know that before I meet you, I had begun to think that I was destined to be alone forever. For my entire life it seemed like the ones that I allowed in, that I loved and valued the most, always somehow deserted me. It all started with my mother when she ran out on me and my father. Her abandoning us scarred me more then I was able to understand at the time. My father had done everything in his power to help heal me of that and just when I was beginning to cope with it my father was snatched away from me. I was young and an orphan when I was sent to live with grandparents who never wanted me around to begin with. They used to look at me with eyes of disgust and contempt. I wasn't able to last there 6 months before they sent me off to foster care. While in foster care I bounced from caretaker to caretaker up until I turned 17 and became fed up with the situation and decided to run away. I had known that in a year's time that I would be 18 and would be able to access parts of the trust fund that was left to me by my father. That year was a long one, but I endured and immediately once able to access my trust I paid for college. Through my college years I went through several relationships, always giving more of myself then I received in return. Even after college most of my relationships gave the same results. I didn't or couldn't at the time understand what was wrong with me. That's when I decided to make one of the biggest decisions of my life at the time and that was to seek counseling in order to try figuring out why I couldn't seem to maintain a lasting relationship. Through counseling I learned of the abandonment issues that plagued me. I came to understand that I had what they refer to as 'Mother issues' and this was the reason why I was so eager to cling to my woman and the reason why I was easily attached. Through this counseling I became stronger and less dependent on relationships that held no real substance. I grew to be in a solid place in my life mentally and physically. I was ready to take on the world!" stated Arnold with much conviction. He continued, "That's when I was invited to attend the potluck for influential African Americans. I remember standing in the midst of three dedicated professionals discussing the politics of the world when I seen the most beautiful woman I'd ever seen in my life. I can still remember the way you walked as if you were gliding. I remember the way your hair laid perfectly down your back and the way your attire hugged your curves as if they were made just for your body. I remember thinking to myself 'there she is...that's the woman for me.' I still remember approaching you that night with some frivolous conversation and I can remember the look that you had in your eyes. That look caused my heart to long for you because the look that your eyes held was the same one that I seen every day as I looked myself in the mirror.

You looked like you were in desperate need to be taken care of. You looked as if you were in desperate need to be considered, to be held, and to be loved. At that moment I had made it a point to myself that I'd be that person for you no matter what it took." Arnold paused briefly before continuing. "Even after everything that we've been through, not once did I doubt my initial intentions. Not once did it ever cross my mind to abandon you because even in your state of confusion, I was 100 percent certain. Now through that certainty I have you for the remainder of my life," Arnold finished before pulling Erica even closer into him.

Erica felt a tear slide down her face as she reflected on everything that Arnold had just relayed to her. She not only knew that Arnold was sincere in what he'd said but she felt it through his touch and witnessed it through his actions. She gathered her composure before whispering thank you to him in appreciation.

"No," Arnold replied. "Thank you," he stated as their limo pulled up to their rented condo they'd reserved for their first night as Mr. and Mrs.

"Enough of the heavy," said Arnold as he climbed out the back of the limo, he grabbed ahold of Erica and swooped her into his arms carrying her into the condo. Erica released a squeal of delight as Arnold carried her inside. Once inside Arnold carried her over and laid her out onto the king-sized bed. He crawled along the bed with her and began planting soft, warm and passionate kisses upon her lips. The exchange began to get heated right before Erica stopped him.

"Hold on baby," said Erica as she scooted from underneath him. She jumped up and headed toward the bathroom.

"Wait where are you going?" asked Arnold in disappointment. Erica swirled around on her heels before leaning up against the bathroom door.

"Don't worry Mr. trust me, you won't be disappointed," she said before closing the door behind her.

Arnold took the time to undress himself completely and laid back out against the headboard with his muscular chest, six pack abs and hardened manhood on full display. Five minutes later the bathroom door finally opened and out stepped Erica. The sight of her made Arnold manhood react automatically. She stood before him in a white sheer thong with matching heels holding only a whip that had a black feather attached to the end of she began taking small and slow steps toward Arnold, lightly rubbing the whip up and between her moist legs. She swirled around delicately giving him a view of her plumped ass before looking over her shoulders mischievously at him. She began swaying her hips from side to side, putting on a hypnotizing show for him. Slowly she turned back around and dropped down into a squatting position. She brought herself back up before quickly dropping back down. Arnold watched in awe as he became extremely aroused by the show that his wife was putting on for him. Erica was on all fours as she began slowly crawling her way toward the bed. She arched her ass up in the most seductive manner, when she made it to the bed, she stood up finally directly in front of Arnold. She began rubbing the whip up his leg letting it rub gently against his manhood before gliding it over his six pack and letting it sit against his chest. She slowly crawled up alongside the bed with him before she cradled his body. Once her hot and moist pussy lips rubbed against him a tingle shot instantly through both of their bodies causing them to lose all control. Erica leaned down and sucked Arnolds lips into her mouth in a rough, forceful, and desired kiss. She felt Arnold's strong hands begin to grip her firm ass as she began grinding herself into him. The friction brought a heat wave in between her legs. Slowly she lifted herself up, grabbing ahold of his manhood she guided him into her with one quick motion. Sitting down onto him gently she allowed herself to become adjusted to him as he filled her up. She enjoyed the mixture of pressure, pleasure, and pain which caused her body to involuntarily shake in ecstasy.

"Ride it like you own it," was Arnold's response to the look in Erica's eyes. She rose slowly before slowly bringing herself down onto him. She gyrated her hips before bringing herself back up again, repeating her motion over and over again until she was bucking against him like he was a thorough bred horse. The sounds of her passion-filled moans filled the room as she began to ride him faster and faster until finally, she exploded in an earth-shattering orgasm that released everything she had inside of her. Simultaneously, Arnold exploded inside of her. Exhausted, Erica laid upon her husband's chest and he wrapped her inside his arm before they both closed their eyes and drifted off into a peaceful sleep.

Chapter Seventeen

Kyle

Kyle sat in the leather cushioned seat of the first-class flight to South Korea with his headphones in listening to R&B. He was deep into thought, about not only his important meeting that he was set to attend but also about everything that he'd been through over the past 7 months. He unconsciously reached over to rub his left shoulder where he was struck with a bullet. The pain was no longer physical, but it remained emotional. He still found himself thinking about his situation with Erica and what led up to the day that he almost lost his life. He'd admitted to himself in that time that he deserved everything that he received that faithful day. Since that time, he'd engrossed himself mostly into work, not allowing any time for social events. He hadn't seen Big Momma or Louis since his release from the hospital. He felt so bad, not for himself, but for Big Momma. The petrified look she had in her eyes when she seen him hooked up to all the machines nearly broke his heart because he'd known that her heart was aching in return. Big Momma didn't leave his side the entire time. While she was there Big Momma asked question after question because she didn't believe in the story that he'd told about the intruder. Big Momma wasn't the only one that didn't believe the story. Louis had known him his entire life and he also didn't believe the story. Louis felt angered and even though he wasn't the violent type he would go to the ends of the earth for his family and friends; he just couldn't figure out who Kyle was trying to protect and why. Since the hospital, Kyle could count on one hand how many times he'd talked to the two.

Kyle glanced to his left and out the window of the plane down at the passing clouds that they were soaring over after a while he turned back to his right 'thinking he had heard someone trying to gain his attention. He removed his headphones from his ears and looked into the eyes of the stranger. "Excuse me," he said, "were you talking to me?" he asked the woman.

"Yes, I said the world looks so much different from the sky, it makes me feel like a part of everything below but detached from it all at once," the lady finished.

"I've never really reflected on it," replied Kyle. "So, exactly what were you reflecting on because you seemed to be someplace else as you stared out the window," enquired the woman. Kyle didn't reply right away. He really didn't know how to respond to the complete stranger that was intruding into his deepest thoughts. The look on his face must have conveyed his thoughts and the woman began to apologize. "I'm so sorry if I'm imposing which is really rude of me considering that I've yet to introduce myself. The name Zoe Fields, and everyone calls me Zoe," introduced the woman while extending her hand out to Kyle for a handshake. Kyle looked down at her hand which was a shining pearly white before he accepted it for a sensual handshake. "Kyle Malone," he replied. "And everyone calls me Kyle," he finished as he looked into the woman's earth tone green eyes. There was something about her eyes that captivated him. He allowed himself to quickly survey her and noted how her silky blond hair cascaded gently down her shoulders. Her delicate lips seemed to be made just for kissing. His eyes went down to her plump and rounded breast that accentuated her business attire perfectly. He found himself becoming slightly aroused once he glanced over her long and lovely legs that was crossed in her light grey business suit. He brought his eyes back up into hers and felt slightly guilty from the lust his eyes gave off.

"Well, since we're not complete strangers anymore maybe you can answer my question now," said Zoe.

"I'm sorry, exactly what was your question again?"

"I was asking what you were reflecting so hard on while staring out the window?" Kyle looked into her eyes before he responded. It was something about the way she asked him that seemed genuine and made him want to be honest with her. He stared into her eyes a second longer then he had intended to before finally replying.

"I was thinking about how life could change so suddenly, one minute you could be up in the sky and then the next you could be on the ground."

"Sounds like a man that has either a lot of promise for the future or a lot of regrets from the past."

Kyle looked at the woman with even more interest now. Not only was she extremely attractive, but she seemed to be very observant as well. Again, he took his time before replying. He no longer felt the need to be reserved but instead felt like opening up.

"A little bit of both," he simply replied.

"One more than the other? asked Zoe.

"Regret," Kyle replied more sadly than he had intended to.

Now it was Zoe's time to pause before responding. Kyle quickly diverted his eye contact from her because he felt more vulnerable than he cared to. Finally, Zoe responded "Love, huh?" she asked giving Kyle an intense and curious look.

"What about love?"

"A love that you regret?"

"Isn't it always?" Kyle replied fully, showing his vulnerability.

"Attention, passengers. Please fasten into your seat belts and prepare for landing," announced the pilot over the loudspeaker, interrupting Kyle's conversation with Zoe.

After the announcement was made, there were no more words exchanged between the two until the flight had completely landed. After preparing to depart, the plane, the two walked side-by-side through the terminal.

"So, what are you doing here in South Korea?" asked Kyle.

"I'm here on business. I leave in a few days on another trip to Tokyo."

"Well, maybe we'll cross paths again while here," replied Kyle. "Yeah...maybe..." finished Zoe as they went their separate ways.

Cante & Louis

"Heeeyyy Chilli!!" exclaimed Big Momma, after opening the door for Louis and Cante. She greeted Louis with their customary hug before he gave her a light peck on the cheek.

"Hey Big Momma," Louis replied before he stepped aside to give Big Momma her first view of Cante.

"Oh, Louis who is this beautiful young woman?" asked Big Momma with true awe of Cante's beauty.

"Big Momma, this is my very, special lady friend, Cante, that I've been telling you about and Cante, this is Big Momma," Louis placed his hand on the small of Cante's back in the most affectionate way after the introduction.

"It's nice to finally meet you Big Momma," stated Cante before stepping up to Big Momma, hand extended.

"Oh, Chilli, if you are here at my home with Louis than you are deserving of much more than a handshake. Come here, Chilli," stated Big Momma before bringing Cante into her with a motherly hug.

Louis stood back with a smile on his face. This would be the first time he'd introduced a woman to his Big Momma. Seeing Big Momma's reaction to Cante gave him a warm feeling inside, a feeling that he had never felt before.

"Come on now, the two of you need to take off those jackets and make yourselves comfortable. Cante, I hope you haven't eaten yet because your Big Momma has a table filled with food prepared. Not sure if Louis told you, but you won't be able to leave this house until you've tasted a little bit of it all," informed Big Momma.

"Trust me, Big Momma, we left plenty of room for your meal, I've informed her about how you are concerning your meals," replied Louis.

"Good. Now I'm going to go finish setting things up in the kitchen, make sure the two of you wash your hands. And then meet me at the table," finished Big Momma as she wobbled her way back into the kitchen.

"Oh my, Louis, she is truly something else," said Cante once Big Momma was out of earshot.

"I told you," Louis replied before laughing more to himself. "You haven't seen anything yet."

"Uhm, uhm, uhm," replied Cante with a chuckle before following Louis to get prepared for dinner. After discarding their jackets and washing their hands, they made their way into the kitchen with Big Momma who was setting the final dishes at the table.

"Come on now, take a seat. Trust me when I say it, the food is much better when it's hot," stated Big Momma jokingly.

Cante and Louis got settled at the table and after grace was said Big Momma took the time to place as much food as she could on their plates. The three of them enjoyed their meal mostly in silence. After they devoured the main courses, Big Momma brought out the desert. The threesome sat and talked while enjoying Big Momma's infamous Banana pudding.

"Are you from here in Chicago?" Big Momma asked Cante.

"No, I'm from a very small town in the state of Minnesota named Minnetonka. But as a child, my parents separated, and my father migrated here to Chicago. So, growing up I'd visit here a lot."

"What is it you do for a living, chilli?"

"Well, I'd hate to sound simple or spoiled but I haven't had to work a labor job since the age of twenty-one. My father owns several casinos which I'm automatically issued a rather large monthly sum. But, on occasion, I do take up modeling gigs for recreation, so I don't consider it a career but rather a hobby," replied Cante.

"Big Momma, Cante is being modest. She just landed a 15-shoot contract with the makeup conglomerate Maybelline," informed Louis with admiration in his voice.

"Oh, Chilli, modeling is befitting of you seeing how amazingly beautiful you are," complimented Big Momma.

"Oh, thank you Big Momma" blushed Cante. Big Momma began to stare a focused stare at Louis which made him feel slightly un-comfortable. "What?" asked Louis of Big Momma's stare.

"Chilli, I've known you since you were twelve years old and have never met one of your acquaintances. Also, I've never seen you look at any woman the way that you are looking at this beautiful chilli. Your face glows and your mouth automatically smile while looking at her. I believe that you might finally be experiencing the Lord's greatest blessing."

"And what is that Big Momma?" asked Louis.

"Love, chilli."

Cante looked over at Louis who looked back over at her. "You see, chilli, love is like a rare treasure that's been hidden beneath the depths of the sea. A treasure that you'll never find until you take a dive into the waters without reservation or fear. You have to have a strong desire to conquer this mystery called love. Once you take that dive and retrieve the treasure, the entire world will begin to look differently to you from that point on."

Cante looked from Big Momma to Louis trying to capture his reaction to Big Momma's words. Louis sat with a concentrated look as he grasped Big Momma's words...

"Now chilli," continued Big Momma, "This treasure that you've discovered will not be filled with gold alone. Inside, you'll find rubies, you'll find silver, and you'll find bronze. The rubies will be your magical moments. These will be the times that your knees seem to go weak just from the sight of the one you love. The times when you can't stand to be apart for too long because your heart won't be able to stand it. Then you'll have your silver moments. These will be the times that love seems to be routine. When that new love or honeymoon phase passes and your trying to figure out what's next. Yes, there will still be great and wonderful times in these silver moments, but there will also be plenty of tests. There will be misunderstandings, confusion, and even hurt... Then there's your bronze moments. In your bronze moments you'll find yourself wondering what the hell are you doing with this crazy person. You'll probably at times feel as though the love isn't there anymore.

You'll argue, you'll fight, or even separate. But chilli, it's in these bronze moments where the true test lies. It's in these bronze moments that you must have courage, faith, loyalty, and trust in one another. These bronze moments are just the set up for greater ruby moments. That's love chilli and when it's true it conquers all."

After Big Momma finished the room fell to a deathly silence. Both Louis and Cante sat reflecting on what Big Momma had just said. Eventually, the conversation diverted and switched several more times throughout the evening before Big Momma informed the two that she no longer had it the way that she used to and was calling it a night. Before she retired, she made sure to tell Cante that it was a pleasure meeting her and asked her to please be gentle with her chilli's heart. She said that she would be sure to and after they exchanged hugs, Louis and Cante made their way back out to his car out front.

"Thank you so much for introducing me to your Big Momma," began Cante as they leaned on Loui's car. "Now, I see why you admire her and where you get so much wisdom from," stated Cante.

"When I'm confused or lost about anything, she is usually who I find my way to. She always seems to have the right answers. Even when they aren't the answers that I want to hear, I know they're the ones that I need to hear."

"You are so blessed to have someone like that in your life."

"Now I'm blessed twice because I have you in my life as well."

"Awww, look at you tryna run your game," joked Cante as they both began to laugh.

"No, I mean it," stated Louis once their laughter subsided.

"I know you do handsome and I feel as though I'm blessed as well."

"I was wondering if you didn't have plans for the next two weeks, I'd love it if you would join me on vacation."

"Actually, I don't have anything planned so I'd love to join you."

"Okay but let's get up on out of here before these Chicago police start harassing us," finished Louis before they got into his coupe and sped off.

*****

Kyle pulled up inside the company's limo to the seventy-story glass tower that the World National Bank occupied in South Korea. He was in for another intense meeting with the entire financial team of World National and it had him on edge, that paired with the fact that he was running twenty minutes late did little to ease that anxiety. He quickly made his way out the limo grabbing his briefcase and hastily making his way inside and up to the forty-fifth floor where the meeting was being held. He took a second to regain his composure and straighten his attire before sneaking into the dimly lit conference room. The only light illuminating was that of the projection screen being used to give examples from the financial analyst who had the floor. Kyle swiftly made his way over to a seat that Alu had reserved for him. Once seated, Alu leaned in and whispered, "Long night, huh?"

"You could say that," Kyle whispered in response.

"You didn't miss much," ended Alu as he refocused on the speaker.

Kyle began to listen in as well, "So, in final, this year has been one of the best in our twenty-year history, revenue-wise for our South Korean chapter. I have copies of all final reports that I'll be emailing to everyone ASAP. Let's keep up the good work!!" finished the man before handing the floor back over to Mr. Collins.

"Okay, everyone, now that's what good strategizing gets us, record breaking numbers in revenue and a decrease in liabilities and expenses. Now, I'll hand the floor over to the person who teaches us how to bring more clients to World National and that's the head of our South Korean marketing department, Ms. Zoe Fields," announced Mr. Collins.

Kyle's body seemed to tense up from hearing the familiar name. He tried to get a good view of the woman that was gracefully making her way up to the front of the conference room but couldn't, due to the dim lighting.

"Hello, ladies and gentlemen," began the woman before she made her way all the way to the front of the room.

Once there, she finally turned toward the attendees giving Kyle a full view of her. His heart seemed to skip a beat from the sight of the beautiful woman that he'd encountered the day prior. He admired the woman's composure, posture, and command of the room. She led the group full of seasoned professionals including bankers, investors, and accountants. Kyle couldn't look away from her and found himself captivated for the second time in less than twenty-four hours by this woman. He sat in awe while she continued to speak but her words became a blur just as well as the rest of the meeting as he sat staring at Zoe. Once the meeting wrapped up, all of the attendees gathered in a separate meeting while sipping expensive wines and enjoying hors d'oeuvres. Kyle watched as Zoe maneuvered around the room, engaging in the extensive conversation with several individuals. Once he noticed that she was alone for the first time, he approached her.

"Zoe Field's," he said while standing tall in front of her. "I guess our paths crossed sooner than we had both expected," he finished with his best smile.

"I guess so, Mr. Malone," replied Zoe while looking Kyle in the eyes. "I didn't know you were the lead accountant for not only the South Korean department but for World National as a whole," she stated, impressed by the position.

"Yes, and I didn't know you were the marketing director for the U.S.," he replied.

"I guess we both found out something new today," replied Zoe softly.

A brief silence overtook their area as an unmistakable energy of attraction consumed them.

"So, where are you staying while you are here?" Kyle asked, clearing the silence.

"I'm staying at the Marriott Hotel about twenty minutes from here, why do you ask?"

"Because I was wondering if you didn't have to be back anytime soon, I know of a fabulous restaurant not too far from here that plays excellent music and serves really good food if you wouldn't mind to grab a bite to eat."

Zoe took a second to bite her lip while looking up into Kyle's eyes before she responded, "I'd love to."

"Let's get out of here," said Kyle before gently grabbing Zoe's hand and leading her away.

Thirty minutes later, Kyle and Zoe sat at a private table enjoying some BBQ seasoned meats while laughing and talking. Rome's 'I Belong to You' played in the background.

"So, Kyle, I'm curious to know what the story is behind all of the hurt that I see in your eyes," Zoe asked after a while.

"How do you know there's hurt in there?" asked Kyle before taking a drag of his Corona.

"Because I, too, once hid the same hurt, so I'm familiar with it replied Zoe.

"So, are you going to tell me?" she asked again.

Kyle took a minute before replying. "I guess I'll begin by admitting that I once deceived and manipulated someone who meant a lot to me. That deception and manipulation caused that person to depart from my life," stated Kyle.

"I appreciate you giving me the short version," began Zoe, "but I was really hoping for the elaborated version, considering the night is young. We have no place else to be," stated Zoe.

Kyle couldn't help but smirk. He had to admit that this woman had a way with words and persuasion. Slowly, he began to relate what all he had been through with Erica. From getting caught cheating, to her running off and him not being able to get over her. He told her about the dreams and of his talk with Big Mamma. He told her about the gifts and about seeing Erica on her birthday into the night at the club. He told her about Arnold showing up at Swiss Accounts and of the warning he gave to leave Erica alone. He told her about the way himself and Erica continued to creep. Finally, he told her about the night Arnold burst into his condo. He told her about him being shot. This was the first time he'd told anyone about the actual events of that night. After Kyle was done, he found himself choking up in his explanation when Zoe scooted her chair around the table closer to him and placed her hand gently upon his.

"In life we all make mistakes, but those mistakes don't make us bad people, they make us human. Universal laws state that everything happens for a reason and nothing just happens. I recognize and sympathize with your pain because your pain was once mine," stated Zoe.

"What is your story?" asked Kyle of Zoe.

Zoe didn't respond right away but stared Kyle in the eyes intently. For the first time Kyle saw vulnerability inside Zoe's eyes. Instantly, he wanted to protect her for some reason. Slowly, she began to speak.

"I've never told this story to anyone before but...his name was Wayne, he was my high school sweetheart and my first love. After high school we both attended the same University in Wisconsin. In our second year of college we decided to get married. After we graduated, we decided he would proceed with a career and we got pregnant with a beautiful little girl named Sasha. Once Sasha turned two, we decided that I would pursue my career as well. Things were going well, and I began to excel in marketing rather quickly and promotions came to me repeatedly. Wayne's career as a professor of history became second to my ambitions and we decided that he would stay at home to give Sasha a permanent figure there while I continued to pursue my ambitions. Promotions continued to come, and my time became limited, and I rarely had time to make it home. From constant meetings in the states and overseas my visits to see Wayne and Sasha were rare. This began to put a strain on my relationship and when I was home. Wayne and I mostly argued. He felt as if I was neglecting them and I felt like he was acting like some type of martyr for sacrificing his career for Sasha. He said things, I said things, and the situation turned toxic to the point that my rare home visits became non-existent." Zoe paused briefly as if she needed to gather her thoughts, she then continued, "His name was Frank, he was the head of marketing for my firm at the time. We traveled together a lot while on business. I began to connect with him not only emotionally but sexually as well." Zoe paused again, taking the time to look Kyle in the eyes for any sign of judgement being passed, after finding none she continued, "He was a powerful man. He was sure, confident, arrogant, and in due time he proved to be an asshole. Still, until this day I'm not sure why I chose him to share my most intimate secrets with, but I did... It was at a company dinner that Wayne and I attended that Frank felt the need to tell Wayne everything that had been transpiring between the two of us. I could still see the hurt in Wayne's eyes. It was like his heart was being ripped right out of his chest. I don't know why, maybe it was because I was a coward, but I just remembered running. I just left the party and ran and didn't stop running. I made my way out of town and refused to answer any of Wayne's phone calls. I received the call at 2 AM on a Sunday morning." Zoe paused briefly as a tear slid down her face. Now it was Kyle's time to offer her comfort as he laid his arm gently across her shoulder, giving her the strength to continue.

"It was a coroner saying that there had been an accident." Zoe paused again as the tears continued to stream down her face. "He said that Wayne had been drunk driving, with Sasha in the car and... and... they didn't make it. They didn't make it. Kyle, it was all my fault because he was drunk driving out looking for me. They were looking for me because all they wanted was for me to come home. I lost my husband and child because of my own selfish motives," finished Zoe as she sobbed into Kyle's chest. Kyle just held her tight and she allowed it all to come out. He didn't say anything because he understood that sometimes there were no words that could heal a situation. They both continued to sit in the diner, Kyle with his arm around Zoe and Zoe lost in her own thoughts. "I'm ready to go back to my hotel," Zoe finally stated. "Okay. Let's go," replied Kyle as they got up and made their way out of the restaurant. Once they made it to Zoe's hotel, Kyle walked her up to her room. Zoe didn't enter her room but leaned her back up against the door as Kyle stood silent before her.

"Kyle, I don't want to be alone tonight," Zoe softly said with her eyes cast down at the ground below. "Okay," he replied softly. "I don't want you to think this is an invitation at sex but rather an invitation for you to hold me tonight," Zoe stated vulnerably. "I promise that is exactly what I'll do," Kyle assured. Zoe turned and slipped the key inside the slot allowing them to enter. After discarding their shoes, they both climbed inside the bed. Zoe snuggled herself into Kyles arms and closed her eyes. All she wanted at the moment was to be held, to not be alone and to not feel neglected and that's exactly what Kyle gave her.

Cante & Louis

Cante and Louis laid out on the patio of Louis yacht while sailing the Pacific Ocean. They were on their final day of their vacation and they wanted to be away from the rest of the world for it. Cante had her leg splayed out over Louis' and her face planted gently against his chest. She looked up at Louis and tried concentrating on the discussion they were having but she found herself distracted by her thoughts of how far along the two of them had come over the last year. She thought back on how they both had initially said that they would probably never find satisfaction in dating only one person. They were now in their sixth month of dating each other almost exclusively. The thought brought a smile to her face. She was amazed at how Louis had changed over the months. How he had went from being reserved, to occasionally showing emotion to her. She was also amazed at how far she had come. With Louis, she had broken some of her cardinal rules and even allowed him to take control more often than not. She had always been skeptical of allowing a man to take control because most men misunderstood that and became controlling. Louis, however, handled it just right. She had to admit to herself that all of these new feelings that she was experiencing were amazing. She trusted herself with Louis and most importantly, she trusted Louis.

"Cante! Cante!" Louis repeated, breaking Cante from her reverie.

"I'm sorry Louis, what did you say?"

"I said, if necessary, we'll have to sign a written contract," repeated Lou.

"A written contract about what?"

"Were you not listening to anything that I was saying? I said that if we make this thing official a brother needs a guarantee on how much loving he's going to be receiving."

Cante began laughing at Louis' statement.

"Louis, you can't be serious, we are not about to sign a love making agreement."

"We have to come to some understanding, because I've heard about how women like to turn nun after commitment," stated Louis seriously.

Again, Cante found herself laughing at Louis' comment. She slapped him lightly on the chest before replying, "That is so not true, you really need to stop listening to people."

"You can't blame a brother for trying to secure himself."

"Okay, Okay, Okay, Louis. I'll be willing to sign your little contract if you would be willing to sign mine," challenged Cante seductively.

"Let me hear it," challenged Louis even more seductively.

Cante brought her lips up to Louis' ear and began to whisper. Slowly, she began to slip her hand inside his swim trunks as she finished what she had been whispering.

"Uhmmm..." Louis hissed from her touch, "as you can feel that would never be a problem," he responded.

"So, with me signing your contract and you signing mine, are you saying that we are officially a couple?" she asked.

"Of course," responded Louis.

The breeze coming from off the ocean sent chills through both of their bodies as Cante suddenly eased up Louis body and began cradling him.

"So, you are saying that you're getting rid of your little black book and that I should do the same?" Cante purred while grinding her body into Louis' and looking him deeply in his eyes. Slowly, she reached behind herself and unleashed the string of her bikini top, letting her breasts catch his attention.

Louis slowly and hypnotically nodded in agreement.

Cante leaned down and began kissing him passionately while continuing to grind her pelvis into his. Louis found himself becoming extremely aroused. Swiftly, he lifted Cante, turning her over and taking control.

"Always have to take control, huh?" Cante purred again.

Louis responded with soft kisses trailing over Cante's exposed breasts. She gasped several times from the delightful feeling. He allowed his strong hands to roam over her soft body. His lips trailed down to the bottoms of her bikini. Swiftly, he pushed it aside and placed a sudden kiss against her moist pussy. She gasped in response to the feeling. Carefully, he continued to lick, bite and nibble on her. She reached down and placed a hand on top of his head, pushing his tongue deeper inside of her. The sensation was so good that she felt herself losing control. Next, he allowed his fingers to take her nipples in between them, flicking and twisting them perfectly. Cante began to moan much louder, surrendering all control over to him. Her legs shivered and shook, and her head went involuntarily from side to side. She felt her body begin to release the juices held within and she began orgasming in ecstasy. Louis slowly made his way back up, kissing Cante firmly upon her lips. He felt her pulling at his swim trunks and he allowed them to come down. He reached his hand down, grabbed ahold of himself and guided himself deep inside of her. Slowly, tenderly, and methodically he began to make love to her just the way she'd whispered to him earlier.

*****

Erica was pacing back and forth in her bedroom. She had a lot on her mind as she waited for Arnold to make it home. He had just finished up a week's long business trip and she had expected him home any minute now. She had rehearsed what she would say to him over one hundred times but still didn't think she had the right words. It had been two months since their honeymoon in Belize and it had also been over a month since her last menstrual cycle which led her to take a pregnancy test. The first results were positive, which made her retake it three more times to be certain; each time produced the same results. She heard the downstairs door open, then close. She began to straighten her hair and check her image in the mirror. She heard Arnold begin to ascend the stairs when she ran to sit at the edge of the bed, hiding the pregnancy test in her pocket.

"Hey baby!" said Arnold once he entered the room. He made his way over to Erica and planted a kiss on her forehead. "What's the matter with you?" he asked of the worried look on her face.

"I have something that I wan... I mean I have something that I need to tell you..." Arnold looked her over and concern instantly etched on his face. A million different things began to run through his mind. He sent a silent prayer up to the Man above in hopes that she wasn't terminally ill or no one they loved suffered an ill fate. Slowly, he sat down next to her while looking into her eyes. "Tell me what's wrong."

"Well, I wouldn't say that something is wrong, I'm just not sure it's something that you are ready for," stated Erica before pulling the pregnancy test out of her pocket and handing it to Arnold.

Arnold looked at the pregnancy test, he couldn't understand it but figured it must've read positive from Erica's reaction. "We're pregnant?" he asked Erica. "Please Erica baby tell me that we're about to have a child," stated Arnold with excitement.

Erica shook her head yes in confirmation. "YES!! YES!! YES!!" Arnold yelled out in excitement and celebration. He stood up, took Erica in his arms and as he lifted her up, he hugged her tightly before spinning her around in circles. "YES!!! This is excellent news!" Arnold finished before sitting Erica back to her feet. He kissed her again several more times before he went down to his knees. He hugged her tightly around the waist once there and put his head into her stomach. A flood of different emotions hit him all at once and he find himself not being able to control himself. The realization of actually becoming a father made him think of his own father. He wanted to be a great man to his child as his father once was to him. A tear of joy slowly slid down his face, he felt Erica's hand roam over the top of his head in a comforting way. Slowly, he looked up into her eyes and noticed several tears staining her face.

"Erica," Arnold began, before making his way to his feet, "tell me whatever you need of me to make this entire process as easy as possible for you. If you need me to take off from work I will, if you need me to be at your beck and call then I'm there. Whatever I have to do to make sure that you have a carefree pregnancy and that you and my child are healthy then that's what I'm going to do," finished Arnold reassuringly. Erica couldn't find any words to say she just began to hold and hug her husband tightly.

"I promise to you Erica that I'll be a great father and continue to be a great husband."

"I know you will," replied Erica while holding her husband tight in her arms.

Chapter Eighteen

Cante & Louis

"Welcome to the most relaxing and sexiest creation I've made to date. This here is my home away from home, my sanctuary and my joy, I call it 'Sweet wonders,'" stated Louis proudly to Cante.

They were in Las Vegas for the weekend and Louis wanted Cante to see the place that he built strictly for his entertainment and desire for adventurous sex. The structure of the establishment was larger and more elegantly laid out then Cante had expected. Sweet wonders was the size of a mini-mansion. Louis had it designed into three separate sections. The first was the massage parlor where one could receive a magnificent and innocent massage. The second section was the brothel where you choose the men or women that you decided to do whatever you would like with. The final section was dubbed the 'Sex playhouse.' Here you could fulfill some of your wildest and kinkiest desires with like-minded individuals.

"This is really nice," complimented Cante as they stood in the lobby admiring the layout.

Just then two hostesses simultaneously approached them, "Hello Louis, how are the two of you doing- today?" they asked.

"We're fine thanks for asking," replied Louis

"Would you like any special accommodations to be made of your private suite this evening?"

"Yes. The only thing that I request if for both Josephine and Symone to be summoned up as our personal masseuse this evening," ended Louis, sending the hostess about their way.

Louis guided Cante up to his private suite. Once there, Cante was once again amazed by how elegantly laid out it was. The suite was dimly lit. The makeshift waterfall sent a peaceful sound throughout the suite as it fell gracefully into a small pond. To the left of the suite was a see-through curtained off section with a bed twice the size of a king-sized bed. The bed rotated slowly in circles as the glass mirrors that surrounded it reflected its movements. There was also a large kitchen, two bathrooms equipped with Jacuzzi's inside and four massage chairs lined up outlooking the lit city streets.

"This is really tasteful," complimented Cante.

"Thank you," replied Louis before continuing, "Let's make ourselves at home and prepare for our masseuse. I have to warn you now that these two are two of the best masseuse on this side of the globe," stated Louis while undressing himself. Cante followed suite and got undressed before making her way to get comfortable in a massage chair next to louis. She was admiring the view when she heard the door open and Josephine and Symone enter the room. Louis asked for the two beautiful women to retrieve a few shots of Patron for Cante and himself before the women began their massage. After preparing the drinks, the two masseuses made their way over and began to slowly and methodically massage the couple.

An hour into the massage, Cante suddenly requested for her masseuses to end her massage. She got up from her chair and after noticing Louis halfway asleep she whispered into his ear, "I'm curious to see what else this place offers," she stated before making her way out of their V.I.P. section, wearing only a towel.

Louis remained stationed. He smiled to himself at Cante's curiosity. He knew that Cante would want to visit the brothel and sex playhouse. He himself just wanted to see what would pique her interest the most.

Forty-five minutes later, Cante was still gone and Louis decided to finally end his massage session. He made it to his feet and over toward his walk-in shower. After a quick ten-minute rinse off he made his way to find Cante.

Louis walked inside his brothel and asked the head madam whether or not she had seen Cante. She said that Cante was there about half an hour ago. Next, he asked what did Cante take interest in during her visit. The madam informed him that Cante ordered a private show with two Hispanic females. The madam relayed that the three had gotten really heated but nothing sexual happened before Cante departed toward the sex playhouse.

"Thank you," said Louis before making his way out to look for Cante in the sex playhouse. Louis never ceased to be amazed by all of the kinky sex that was taking place there. The sex playhouse section was the place for exhibitionist and voyeur. Whatever your mind could think of sexually it was being role played and put on display.

As Louis walked through, he was offered several invitations to join in on some action, but he denied as he continued to search for Cante. Finally, he noticed Cante from a distance. The sight of her made his manhood stand to attention immediately. Cante was tied up to a leather domination equipment, completely naked. She was being circled constantly by a man holding only a whip. Cante didn't immediately notice Louis but once she did, she gave him the most provocative look he had ever received.

Louis continued toward Cante until he approached her.

"I told him that he could be in control until my master came," whispered Cante seductively to Louis. The man holding the whip walked over to Louis and handed the whip over. Without any words, the man departed.

"You love to be in control, huh?" Cante teased. "You love it when I surrender to you, right? Now you have complete control," finished Cante.

Louis began to prowl around Cante as if she was his prey. It turned him on so much seeing her tied up and in his control. He'd never relayed the fact that he was the dominant type, but the fact that she knew, turned him on even more.

Slowly, Louis began to rub along Cante's body with the whip. The feel of the leather against her skin brought goosebumps to her, Louis began to rub the whip over her hardened nipples. Down through the folds of her pussy lips and over the back of her ass cheeks. Cante breathed in deeply and moaned simultaneously from the feel of the leather. Louis brought the whip up and then down against Cante's soft, round ass with just the right amount of force.

"So, you've recognized that I like to be dominant...I wonder, did you also recognize that I don't like it when something of mine is being handled by someone else?" Louis stated, continuing to prowl around Cante.

"You've allowed yourself to be handled by another man and there are consequences for that," stated Louis before he brought the whip down against Cante's ass once again.

Cante hissed in response to the feeling. The feeling wasn't pain but of pure ecstasy. Louis knew how to do it perfectly. "I didn't know that you wouldn't tolerate it," whined Cante knowingly and seductively.

"Well...now you do!" responded Louis while bringing the whip up and down against Cante's soft ass yet again. Louis continued this process until he felt that Cante was hot in all the right places. Slowly, he began to unhook Cante from her restraints. Once free, she fell into his arms. Louis picked her up and carried her through the crowd of patrons. Cante was never one to be shy about her sexuality or her body. She always felt comfortable in her own skin and at the moment she felt the most comfortable while being carried naked by her man through a house full of people.

Louis carried her back up to their suite and laid her out over the massive bed. Slowly, he climbed on top of it with her. He parted her legs with his legs and with his hands he placed hers above her head and held them therein the most submissive way. Next, he began kissing her passionately and forcefully. She returned his desire equally, moaning into his mouth. She felt like she would cum at any moment from all of the excitement. Louis carefully let his right hand go to his manhood and he guided himself into Cante. Once he did, she gasped loudly and she wrapped her legs immediately around his waist, taking him fully inside of her.

Louis took his time and he timed his strokes perfectly. He wanted her to feel his passion through and through, with every thrust. He wanted her to know that there wasn't a feeling another human could give her that he couldn't also give her. He wanted her to know how deep his love was for her, so he went even deeper with his stroke. He continued making love to her, making sure to caress her, feel her, and touch every piece of her that he could.

Cante began to cry out in ecstasy, she tried bringing her hands down so that she could dig her nails deep into his back, but he held them restrained above her head. She wanted to bite down on his neck, but he wouldn't allow it. He was in complete control, touching the places that she needed him to and hitting the places that drove her crazy.

Finally, she began to scream out as everything she had built up inside her came screaming out in an earth-shattering orgasm. Louis let himself subside while still inside of her. He let her hands loose and he kissed her softly on the lips. She wrapped her arm around him, holding him tightly before surrendering herself into a comatose sleep.

*****

Arnold and Erica stood together in front of their new business venture, 'Forever Together' with a human sized pair of scissors in hand. The red ribbon that separated them from the crowd waved slightly with the wind. The attendees mostly consisted of family, friends and future investors. Arnold and Erica had decided to embark on this venture together and allowed Debra to take full acting control of 'Forever United.' 'Forever Together' was designed to give guidance counseling to young couples who faced troubling times in their relationship. 'Forever Together's' goals was to get young couples to understand that the easy route to take was to give up while in a relationship and that it takes more heart and courage to believe in one another. Arnold and Erica felt that their situation wasn't unique as far as the struggles that they once endured and understood that there's plenty of young couples facing some of the same struggles and they wanted to help counsel those couples.

"I want to thank everyone for coming out today for the grand opening of 'Forever Together.' Today marks a new day for those who sometimes get lost while in their relationships because you now have a place to go and counselors to come to for answers. So together, let's all not only allow love to prevail but make it prevail..."

"On the count of three, we'll all cut the ribbon together...1...2...3..." stated Arnold as he cut the ribbon with Erica's help.

The attendees began to clap their hands in celebration of the event. Next, they all began to congregate with one another. Arnold and Erica began mingling in the crowd. Arnold's goal was the meet and talk to some of the potential investors and Erica wanted to seek out some interested couples.

"How are you doing, sir?" asked one of the attendees as he approached Arnold.

"I'm doing fine, sir and how about yourself?" replied Arnold.

"Good. This is a very nice venture you are embarking on. I myself believe in the beauty of young love and helping it overcome the obstacles and strain that society places on them," stated the stranger.

"That's the very reason why we decided to take up this business. Love is powerful and love lost is just as powerful..." The name's Mr. Simmons, by the way..." stated Arnold as he reached out to shake the man's hand.

"Mr. Swiss," replied the man, taking Arnold's hand fully into his own. In the midst of the handshake, a sharp pain suddenly pierced through Arnold's head. He slightly bent over from the pain. Releasing Mr. Swiss' hand.

"Are you okay, sir?" asked Mr. Swiss.

"Yes...Yes...Of course, I'm fine," replied Arnold as the pain began to subside.

"Well Mr. Simmons, I believe in what you are trying to accomplish here, and I am really interested in making a rather large investment," informed Mr. Swiss.

"I believe that you would be making a wise decision in deciding to invest here," said Arnold while handing Mr. Swiss his business card. After today, I'll be accepting conversations concerning investments. If you would like, I will fax to you a copy of our business plan first thing so that you can review it and have a better understanding of the direction that we are headed in before we begin conversations."

"That would be perfect, Mr. Simmons," stated Mr. Swiss before handing Arnold his business card. "It was nice talking to you Mr. Simmons and hopefully we can do business soon," ended Mr. Swiss before extending his hand out to Arnold again. Arnold accepted Mr. Swiss hand for a firm handshake. Again, he was caught off guard by a sharp pain shooting through his head that caused him to double over in pain.

"Mr. Simmons are you okay?" asked Mr. Swiss

"Yes...Yes..." said Arnold as he staggered away from Mr. Swiss. He began looking around for Erica. Once he spotted her, he slightly struggled his way over toward her.

"Arnold are you okay?" Asked Erica noticing the agonizing pain in his eyes.

"No, I'm not sure what's going on, but I keep getting a really sharp pain inside my head.

"Maybe it's because your overwhelmed, would you like to go home and try getting some rest?"

"I think that would be a great idea," replied Arnold. Erica began to wrap things up before leading Arnold to their car. Once they made it home Erica lead Arnold up to their bedroom. She made him comfortable before going to retrieve some pain meds for him to take. After Arnold took the medications Erica slipped into bed with him before they cuddled up and slipped off to sleep.

Arnold & Erica

(Dad, dad is that you? Dad where are you going? You can't leave me here alone dad, I have no one without you... Arnold ran through the smokey streets toward the dark alley. He tried catching up with his father who was slowly walking down the darkened alley suddenly his father stopped. Dad said Arnold Jr. while running up to his father. "Stop son! You cannot come any closer!"... "Why not dad? Dad I need you!" repeated Arnold Jr. as he took a step closer...."No son! You must stop now! If you do not you will be forced to make some tough decisions that could change the course of your life, just turn and leave son. Runaway now while you have the chance." "...But dad I can't, I can't dad because I need you. I need you dad," repeated Arnold Jr. as he reached for his father. Quickly he reached out and turned his father to face him..."Dad! Hey, I know you're not my father! Why do you have my father's voice? Why do you sound like my father, why do you have my father's body and call me son when you're not my father?!?" Questioned Arnold Jr...." "No, I'm not your father...But I killed your father!" replied the man.)

Dream... "Huhuuuhhh!!" screamed Arnold as he awoke from his dream. Erica awoke quickly and tried calming Arnold down. He was sweating profusely all over and tears was running down his face. "Huhhhh!" he continued to scream out in confusion and delusion.

"Baby calm down, you were having a bad dream," Erica said while trying to embrace him. Arnold broke away from her, looking at her like he didn't know who she was. "Baby it's me! You were having a nightmare," consoled Erica. Arnold quickly jumped from their bed and backed himself into a corner. He looked around in a delusional state. He seemed lost and panicked. He broke down into a squatting position and looked around the room from left to right. Quickly, he jumped up and ran out of their bedroom and out of the house.

Erica tried following him, she was stunned and confused. She'd never seen Arnold react in such a way. She made her way downstairs and to the front door. She looked out the door that Arnold left wide open and noticed his car speeding away down the street.

Chapter Nineteen

Cante & Louis

Louis sat reclined on his lazy boy flicking through his flat screen television. He really wasn't one to indulge in watching television but decided to enjoy it a little bit. He was at his condo in New York after locking in a one hundred-million-dollar contract with a distribution chain in Japan and was really feeling good about himself. After tipping back his corona, he began smiling to himself. His thoughts weren't of the major contract but of Cante. Cante had really stolen his heart. Ever since they'd become exclusive, he put his black book away and focused solely on her. He'd never been in love before, but he had no doubt that what he was feeling for her was love. Cante made him so happy and when they were together, they had so much fun. Initially he had to get over his paranoia from her old playa ways and eventually began to trust her and trust himself.

DING DONG...DING DONG....DING DUNG...

The sound of the doorbell broke Lou from his deep thought. He got up and made his way to the door. Sure, that it was Cante, he opened it without asking who was there. "Louis!" said the visitor once the door was opened. "I'm so glad that I caught you here!"

"Janelle! What's up little sister? What are you doing here? Come in! Come in!" repeated Lou in excitement.

"I was traveling through on my way to the Carolinas and thought 'Hell I might as well stop by and see if you were here' I'm so happy that I caught you!" "Yeah, me too. It's been so long," replied Lou as he embraced Janelle in a tight hug. Janelle and Louis' relationship dated back to when they were toddlers. Janelle and Lou's parents were really close friends when they were kids. Janelle's parents ended up succumbing to the addiction of drugs and put her off on Lou's parents. Growing up, Lou was like a big brother to Janelle. He protected her and always made her feel safe. Once they got older, Lou went off to Illinois University and Janelle went on a missionary all throughout Africa. Throughout the years, they tried seeing one another just to catch up but it had been over three years since they last encountered one another. "Go ahead and put your things away, you know where the guest bedroom is," stated Lou. Once Janelle got herself settled in, she joined Lou in the living room. Lou had made them both a few sandwiches along with a few beers. When they were together, they usually enjoyed some beers and reminisced on their childhood. This day was no different.

"I swear you used to be terrified of that Chucky doll," Lou said while laughing out loud at Janelle.

"You used to torture me with that dammed thing. I'd run all over the house, hide in closets, under blankets or whatever I had to do to get away from it," said Janelle while laughing along with Lou. "I bet your still frightened by it, " Joked Lou. "No, I'm not Louis. I'm so over it," stated Janelle as they sat, continuing to talk, joking and laughing. After a while Lou got up and excused himself to get them some more beers. When he returned, he had his hands behind his back with a mischievous smirk on his face.

"Louis, what are you up to?" asked Janelle suspiciously. Louis didn't respond as he continued to proceed toward Janelle. "Louis, what do you have behind your back?" asked Janelle just as Lou walked up on her. Quickly, he pulled the Chucky doll he had behind his back out. "OHHH MY GOD!!" screamed Janelle as she got up and began running away." Louis put that thing away!"

"I thought you said that you were over it?" replied Lou while chasing Janelle around the house with the doll. Janelle found herself running into the kitchen and around the counter trying to evade Louis. Louis continued trying to catch her but found it hard. Suddenly, Janelle picked up a bottle of Ketchup from the counter. "I swear if you don't stop, I'm going to squirt you," threatened Janelle. Ignoring her warnings, Louis continued to chase her. Suddenly, Janelle began squirting Ketchup all over Louis causing him to drop the Chucky doll. "Oh, so that's how we're playing?" asked Louis before grabbing the bottle of Mustard and squirting Janelle with it. Before long, a full-fledged food fight ensued as both Janelle and Louis threw whatever food they could on one another. "Okay, okay, I give," surrendered Louis after a while. He had a mixture of Ketchup, Mustard, sugar, and flour all over him. Janelle looked similar before she stopped. Together, they started laughing again. Louis made his way over to Janelle, putting his arm around her he joked "You smell like you need a shower now little sister." "I know, right?" she agreed. "You do too. While you standing there smelling like a Harold's chicken," she joked and they both laughed again. "You go and shower, and I'll go and take mine. See you afterward," said Louis before making his way to his master bedroom. He quickly undressed and hopped inside the shower. Fifteen minutes later he was out and dressed. He made his way back downstairs to prepare a quick snack for himself and Janelle. Knowing Janelle, he had at least another twenty minutes or so before she got out of her shower. Louis straightened up the kitchen before he brought out his tortilla chips and made a sauce for them to enjoy. Once that was completed, he mixed Janelle a few margaritas just the way she like them. He brought himself out a bottle of whiskey. Making out into the living room he sat the items onto the table. Just then the doorbell began to ring again. The sounding of the doorbell brought a smile to his face. He was sure that it was Cante this time. He made his way to the door and opened it. His smile widened at the sight of his beautiful woman. Cante had her hair laid down her back, make-up applied perfectly with a flower sundress fitting her body loosely. Louis instantly brought Cante into his body for a tight hug and then a kiss" Come in baby," said Louis.

"Oh my, that was one long and exhausting flight," complained Cante as she made it into the foyer. At that same moment Janelle entered the foyer, wearing only her towel that was wrapped around her body and one that wrapped up her hair. "Louis, where's the hair dryer? I looked all over the room and it's not there," said Janelle before she noticed Cante for the first time. "Louis! What the hell is going on here?" asked Cante as she began to back away from Louis.

"This isn't what it looks like Cante," stated Louis, looking back from Cante to Janelle. Cante continued to back pedal before turning to make her way back to the door. "It's always what it looks like," replied Cante as she rushed out of the door. "Wait Cante! Wait! Please allow me to explain," screamed Louis at Cante's back. Cante didn't stop as she made her way down the driveway and into the street. Quickly, she got inside of her rental car and sped off. Louis continued to call out to Cante with no luck. He turned back to find Janelle still standing behind him, "I hope that I didn't get any trouble started," she stated. Louis didn't respond, he just walked right past her and up to his master bedroom.

Kyle & Zoe

Once Kyle had made it back to the States, He continued to engross himself into his work. Before leaving South Korea, he and Zoe exchanged numbers. In that time, they had talked almost daily for hours at a time. When Kyle wasn't working, he was talking to Zoe and the two had begun to become close. Kyle sat behind his oakwood desk at Swiss accounts finalizing the post-closing trial balance for the end of the accounting period. He was almost finished when Susan his receptionist chimed in on his line. "Mr. Malone, there's a Zoe Fields here to see you. I see that she's not booked for an appointment but she's adamant about coming in. Would you like for me to tell her to book an appointment?" asked Susan.

"No, no. It's fine, please send her in," replied Kyle before he stood up to straighten his business suit and run his hands over his waves, making sure his appearance was immaculate.

"Will do," ended Susan.

Kyle made his way around his desk in preparation to greet Zoe. Susan opened the door allowing Zoe inside. Kyle felt a funny feeling sweep through his stomach at the sight of Zoe. He watched as she approached, holding a single red rose inside her hand.

"Hello Kyle, this here is for you," Said Zoe, handing the rose to Kyle. "Thank you. I must admit that this is the very first time I've been on the receiving end of a rose."

"Well, this will be the very first time you've ever been around a woman like myself."

"So, your claiming originality." challenged Kyle.

"I guess you can say that. I just chose the non-customary approach, especially in pursuit."

"In pursuit of what?"

"In pursuit of you," Zoe replied in a seductive way.

Kyle couldn't help but to chuckle at Zoe's bluntness. "That would be another first for me, a woman openly admitting to pursuing me rather than me of her."

"Oh, before I forget," said Zoe while reaching inside of her purse and pulling out a jewelry box. She handed it to Kyle before saying "Open it." Kyle opened the box and was surprised to see a very expensive Richard Millie watch inside.

"That watch was just released, I seen it and thought that it would be a very nice way of thanking you for not taking advantage of me when I was vulnerable."

"Wow," said Kyle before unleashing his Rolex from his wrist and putting on the Richard Millie. "This is another first for me, a woman giving me a gift without receiving one from me first...Thank you," stated Kyle in appreciation.

"Now, do you still question my originality?" asked Zoe flirtatiously. Kyle laughed again at Zoe's response.

"So, Mr. Malone, did I catch you with a busy schedule or do you have time for a quick lunch?"

"I was actually just finishing up in here. What did you have in mind?" questioned Kyle.

"I was thinking about a walk along your city's beautiful Lakeshore and maybe a couple of hot dogs and a coke," stated Zoe.

"I'll tell Susan to clear my schedule for the remainder of the day," said Kyle before grabbing his jacket and leading the way out.

Kyle and Zoe walked alongside Lake Michigan eating hot dogs, sipping sodas, and discussing whatever came to mind.

"Don't tell me that you came to Chicago just for me," Kyle was saying.

"Actually, that's the very reason why I came," confirmed Zoe.

"Well, I'm not worth the trip, trust me," advised Kyle.

"I beg to differ or else I wouldn't be here..." Zoe paused a second before continuing.

"I'm a bit confused though I have to admit," she stated.

"Confused about what?"

"About how a man that is so handsome, intellectual, successful, empathetic, and caring could lack confidence the way that you do."

"It's not confidence that I lack, I believe, it's more lack of faith."

"What is it that you don't have faith in?" questioned Zoe. Kyle contemplated this question before replying. What was it that he lacked faith in? Certainly, it wasn't his career because he excelled in it easily. It wasn't in his looks because he'd never had a problem catching the eye of the opposite sex. *So, what was it?* he questioned. Just then he realized, "I don't have faith in a person's ability to remain true. I don't believe a relationship could last nowadays and I don't believe that love conquers all anymore." Zoe didn't respond right away. She allowed Kyle's words to play in her mind while they continued to walk in silence. The wind coming off the lake chilled her skin. Kyle noticed, and taking off his jacket, he put it over Zoe's shoulders and put his arm around her as they continued to walk. Together they watched seagulls soar dangerously close to pedestrians while trying to snatch whatever scraps that they could from the ground. Finally, Zoe began to speak. "I've been trying to formulate a correct response to your lack of faith but realized that there isn't one. I've already confided into you about being an unloyal wife once upon a time. I told you about how I ruined a union that was destined to last forever. Also, I told you exactly how I ruined the name of love. But I must admit that through it all, I never gave up hope that true love still exists. Nor did I lose faith in my ability to eventually love someone the right way one day. I've always believed that you shouldn't allow one situation to mess up what could be in the future. Whether you were the party in the wrong or whether you were the one that was wronged, you can't lose faith because the moment that you do will be the moment that you miss out on something special and beautiful," Zoe allowed her words to sink in before continuing, "Kyle, when you first rode a bike were you afraid?" "Of course, I was. I was also excited at the same time," replied Kyle. "When you fell in love for the first time did you feel both afraid and excited?" asked Zoe.

"Yeah, amongst other things."

"Your first time falling off a bike, how did it make you feel about riding a bike again afterwards?"

"At first I felt hurt and didn't want to ride again," replied Kyle.

"So, did you ever ride again?"

"Of course."

"What made you try again?"

"The first thing was when I saw all of my friends riding and having fun while I stood on the sidelines watching. The next reason was my poppa telling me that sometimes you have to fall in order to get up, and finally my desire to conquer something that had tried defeating me made me try again."

Zoe and Kyle continued to walk but without words. Zoe again began to reflect on what Kyle said. She found it sorta ironic for him to want to conquer something tangible but continue to fear something intangible and beautiful. Zoe veered off and made her way over to a bench alongside the Navy Pier and sat down. Kyle followed and sat down beside her. She took the time to lean her head against his shoulder and he wrapped his arm around her. Together, they watched as crowds of people came and went. Zoe began watching an elderly couple as they walked hand in hand. The elderly gentleman seemed to have cracked a joke to his spouse and she laughed a hearty laugh. Zoe took a moment to point the couple out to Kyle.

"Look," said Zoe while pointing to the elderly couple," Do you see the smile that she has on her face?"

"Yes," replied Kyle. "They look very happy, don't they?" asked Kyle with a hint of desire in his voice.

"Yes, they do...Am I detecting a slight hint of desire in your voice?"

"I wouldn't say its desire that you hear but I will admit that I do remember a time that I was very happy like that and I sorta miss having that feeling."

"It sucks being on the sidelines and watching others enjoy something that you really want doesn't it?" Zoe asked rhetorically.

Kyle didn't respond because he could see where Zoe was headed with this. She continued, "I don't know but maybe your first time falling off a bike was similar to your first time falling in love. You rode, you fail, you were hurt but you got up. Are you going to allow Love to defeat you or are you going to get up and conquer this Love thing?"

Kyle just looked at Zoe without any words. Zoe got up and proceeded to walk away from Kyle. "Hey," Kyle yelled out to her. "Where are you going?"

"I'm staying at the W, Mr. Malone. Room 110. I'll be in town for three days. Reflect on what I've just said and hopefully I see you again before I leave," she replied as she continued to walk away.

Cante & Louis

"Hello...Yeah, Cante this is Louis. I see I've received your voicemail yet again. I've never been one to leave a voicemail, but I guess there's a first time for everything. I know you probably still don't want to hear me out, but I really wish you would, so you'd understand that this has all been a big misunderstanding. Honestly, I do believe that I deserve for you to at least hear me out. I won't try explaining myself over this voicemail, so I'm hoping that you'll eventually call back so that we could meet up and get an understanding. Well...Hopefully I hear back from you soon. I'll be waiting," finished Louis while sitting at a bar in downtown Chicago. After Louis finished leaving his message, he beckoned the bartender over for yet another round. It been over two weeks since Cante mistakenly assumed that Louis had been cheating on her. He'd called her several times, but she'd refused to answer any of his calls. He found himself feeling ways that he had never before. Lately he'd been lacking the energy to do anything, and it was beginning to affect his business ventures. He'd cancelled several important meetings for very major contracts. Louis was always on top of his game, but lately he'd been at the bottom of it. He threw his shot back and tapped on the bar to gain the bartenders attention, "Two double shots this time Drew," he yelled out. He pulled out his phone and contemplated calling Cante again but thought better of it. 'What the hell,' he said to himself. If this was love and how love would make him feel, then he no longer wanted any parts of it. This had been the first time that he'd taken a chance at monogamy. In his past, he'd played plenty of games with women. He knew all of the tricks of the trade, but as of late he was tired of that lifestyle. He was tired of waking up to different women everyday not even knowing their names. Cante gave him the feeling of being whole. She gave him the feeling of happiness and satisfaction. With her was the first time he'd been up front and open about everything. He began wondering what she'd been up to lately and wondered had she resorted back to her old lifestyle of being a playa. The thought hurt him; he couldn't imagine Cante laying in the arms of another man. He closed his eyes and tried regaining his composure. He got up from the bar and made his way over to the old-fashioned jukebox that sat off to the side in a corner. He inserted a couple of coins then flicked through the available songs. He stopped once he ran across the song 'Incomplete' by Siscio. The song began to boom throughout the bar before Louis made his way back over to his stool.

"Hey Drew, two more double shots," yelled Louis with much more force then what was intended. The bartender made the drinks and brought them over but before handing them to louis he whispered, "you're reaching your limit Louis, I hope you don't plan on driving that fast and expensive car you have sitting out front do you?" Louis looked at Drew with a frustrated look before replying sarcastically, "NO I DO NOT. Now can I please have my shots!" he demanded. The bartender did what he was told. Afterward, Drew made his way to a phone in the back of the bar. He picked it up and dialed a number. When the person on the other end answered, he said, "Hey, this is Drew, I think you might need to get down here. I'm not sure exactly what it is Louis is going through, but he's already surpassed the legal limit to drive and he don't seem close to stopping," Drew relayed.

"I'm on my way," was all the man said. Twenty minutes later Louis was still ordering up rounds. He'd commandeered the jukebox, playing the song 'Incomplete' over and over again. His words had started to become a slur and his actions belligerent. Kyle walked through the door of the bar and made his way over to assist his friend. He sat at the stool next to Louis without Louis even noticing. He placed a hand on Louis's shoulder. "Hey Muther..." Louis began to say before he realized that it was his best friend. "OHHH! What's up Kyle?" Louis shouted out drunkenly. He embraced Kyle in a brotherly hug. "Damn Kyle, where have you been? I've been trying to contact you, Big Momma has been trying to contact you, we've all been trying to get in contact...Wait a minute, wait a minute...don't you tell me that Drew called you up here. You piece of shit Drew...You're a piece of shit you know that?...I'm not a kid, I can handle myself," Louis slurred. "Naw bro, I just so happened to be in the neighborhood. But I'm glad that I caught you, what's going on with you, bro? I haven't seen you this intoxicated since college," stated Kyle.

"She left me. She left me...She's gone bro. I tried, I tried love and it failed me."

"Wait a minute, we're talking about Cante?"

"Yes, Yes, Cante, she's gone. But I did nothing wrong and she left me. I've tried calling, I've tried several times," slurred Louis.

"What happened?"

"Janelle, Janelle is what happened," replied Louis.

"Are you talking about our little sister Janelle?"

"Exactly, exactly, our little sister. Cante thought I'd been cheating with Janelle. Janelle couldn't arouse me after ten years without sex and Cante thought that I had been cheating with Janelle."

"How'd this happen?"

"Janelle was getting out of the shower at my condo in New York when Cante arrived and thought that I was just sleeping with Janelle. How could this be bro? How could it be that I've done everything...I've done everything right by Cante but yet still I'm wrong," Louis stated confused.

"Sometimes Love is confusing that way. You can be right in every way and still be wrong."

"But how could that be? How could this be?" questioned Louis.

"It's because there are no set rules in love. There isn't a guideline that tells you to do it this certain way in order to receive these certain results. There isn't a curriculum. There are no teachers, no classrooms. Love is like walking blindly and hoping that you don't bump your head into something that you'll regret," said Kyle, offering Louis the same advice that he'd once been given. "But I'm not blind, I can see things clearly, so how is it that I'm still lost?" questioned Louis.

"I wish I had the answers. I wish I could give you a road map to the path of love without flaw, but I can't. No one can. It's one big risk. Every time you wake up, everything you say or do. It's all a risk of rather there will be love gained or love lost," counseled Kyle.

"How can she not understand that all I want is her? I don't want Janelle, I don't want anyone but her," said Louis before sitting his head down on the bar in a defeated way.

"I know bro, I understand," said Kyle as he sat a comforting hand on his friend's shoulder.

Slowly Louis lifted his head up and began singing along to the music. The words to the song fit his situation perfectly and it had him emotional. He staggered out of his bar stool and stumbled slightly when he was on his feet. He began to sing the song even louder, gaining the attention of several of the other patrons at the bar. Slowly he began to stumble his way back over to his bar stool. He leaned on Kyle slightly as he spoke, "I'm ready to go home bro. Can you, can you please drop me off at my house because Drew, Fuckin Drew, who knows it all, says that I can't drive... But I'm ready bro because I'm tired, my heart is tired, my soul is tired. I just. I just want to go home and go to sleep. Can you please take me to my house bro?" Louis slurred drunkenly.

"I got you bro," Kyle replied. He put Louis's arm over his shoulder and carried him away from the bar.

Chapter Twenty

Kyle & Zoe

Kyle stood outside of room 110 at the W. He wanted to knock, but hesitated. He'd just dropped Louis off at his home and what Louis was going through had his mind racing. Tonight, he was able to see a different side of his friend. A part that showed Louis actually had a heart for a woman. Throughout their friendship he'd never seen Louis so emotional, especially over a woman. This experience made him realize exactly how powerful love is. Love had the power to completely change a person. One could turn from bad to good or vice-versa, or in his case one could just give up completely. He began to think about his opinion of love now. Had he really given up? If so, why was he standing outside of room one ten? He knew that the woman on the other side of the door desired love still and hinted at sharing it with him. He went to knock but pulled his hand back yet again. Was he really ready to give love another chance? Was he really ready to put his situation with Erica behind him? He thought for several more seconds before determining that yes, yes, he was ready. Lightly he tapped on the door. He tapped several times more before it finally swung open. He looked down at Zoe as she looked up at him. Neither tried speaking, they just stood without saying anything, but saying everything. Finally, Zoe stepped aside, allowing Kyle to enter. Kyle glanced around the hotel room, looking from the Jacuzzi, to the fireplace, over to the bar and finally at the bedroom.

"I'm so glad that you came," Zoe said.

"So am I," replied Kyle.

"You look to have a lot on your mind, would you like for me to fix us up a couple of drinks and we can talk about whatever," stated Zoe.

"That would be nice," replied Kyle before making his way over to sit at the bar. Zoe fixed the two of them a couple of drinks and made her way over to Kyle's side to take a seat. Kyle picked up his drink and took a swig before he began to talk.

"My best friend Louis, I've known him all of my life," he began. "Together we'd been through a lot. In college he was the biggest womanizer on campus. He had his shot at almost any woman, and he managed to conquer most of them. Me, on the other hand, I was the lover boy. I had one woman and that one woman was all I needed. We were the complete opposite in that way. Louis used to ask me why would. I choose just the main course when I had access to the entire buffet," Kyle laughed to himself at the memory. "Louis couldn't seem to understand me and was even more confused when I said that I couldn't understand him. He used to ask "How could you not understand me? I'm living the life," I'd say to him, "Does it ever get tired some not having someone you could share something real with?" He'd respond with, "Does it ever get boring sharing life with only one person?" We couldn't seem to understand one another's viewpoint. Life went on like this for years, me enjoying the stability and comfortability of having someone I felt like I was connected to the soul with and him, enjoying a variety. This was up until recently...Louis had begun to ask me questions about love. Questions about being in love, about making love work, about making a woman feel secure, about relationship etiquette....He had finally fallen in love after thirty-five years of life," said Kyle as he shook his head and took a sip from his drink.

"Well that's a wonderful thing Kyle," Zoe said not completely understanding Kyle's reaction.

Yeah up until tonight...I got a call from a childhood friend of ours that owns the bar that we frequent. He called to inform me that Louis was beyond drunk, that he was acting belligerent, and talking nonsense. He said that I needed to get there quickly. I walked inside the bar and seen my friend who haven't gotten so much as a buzz off liquor since college, pissy drunk. After sitting down with him he began to explain to me that she'd left him, she'd left him with no legit reason as to why. Strictly off of assumption. He said that she refused to answer any of his calls, she wouldn't even give him a chance to explain himself...Now I've known Louis my entire life and this is the very first time I've seen him be faithful to a woman. He went out on a limb and allowed himself to fall in love for the first time and it failed him," stated Kyle as he finished off his drink.

"How do you know that it's the end of their story?" questioned Zoe.

"I don't. Neither does he. All we do know is that right now, love seems to have failed again."

"I believe that everything happens for a reason, there's a bigger reason as to why they're going through what they're going through. Just like I believe there's a bigger reason as to why you just told me this story," stated Zoe to Kyle with a knowing look on her face.

Kyle grabbed his second drink and finished it off before he began to speak. "I have to admit to you Zoe that 1 want to try this love thing again. I mean I need to try it again. I need to know that I could be true to someone. I need to conquer the thing that seems to be un-conquerable. I need to feel like...like, I'm soaring on a cloud to utopia. I need love just as much as anyone, but a part of me is still afraid. A part of me is still afraid of failure and the hurt that love causes." Zoe got up from her stool and walked behind Kyle. She allowed her hands to roam over his neck and onto his shoulders. She massaged his shoulders firmly to try releasing whatever tension that was there. Slowly, she kissed him upon his neck, she let her kisses trail up to his ear. Softly, she whispered into his ear, "I'm afraid too, Kyle, trust me I am. I haven't been in love nor have I so much as pursued a man since my late husband. I've went years sitting on the sidelines afraid to get back in the game. I doubted the person that I know I really am and could be for someone for years. I felt like I was undeserving of someone else's love and felt like I couldn't love adequately. I'm tired of being alone Kyle. I'm tired of feeling inadequate. I'm not telling you that you shouldn't be afraid because I am too. I'm just asking you if we can be afraid together?" Zoe finished before kissing Kyle again lightly on the ear.

Kyle swirled around in his stool to face Zoe. He looked her in the eyes before he began kissing her softly on the lips. She returned his kiss with just a little more passion and desire. Kyle stood to his feet and together they kissed one another ferociously while removing one another's cloths. The exchange made its way into the bedroom before Kyle lifted Zoe onto the bed. Slowly, he climbed onto the bed with her. She opened her legs widely, allowing him to climb in between them. He began kissing her gently on the lips. Their passion and desire filled the room. Slowly, Zoe broke away from their kiss, she looked up into Kyles eye's, the look was one of surrender and vulnerability. She whispered softly," Take care of me please Kyle, take care of my heart." "I promise to you I will," Kyle replied before he slowly entered Zoe. Her moans were like the sweetest music to Kyle's ears. He felt a feeling of complete harmony sweep through his heart as he looked down at Zoe. He knew right then and there that he'd fallen in love with her and he wanted her to feel what he'd just felt. He began making love to her more passionately, allowing her to feel and have all of his love.

*****

Zoe awoke from her sleep and reached over to wrap her arms around Kyle. When her arm fell upon only the pillow, she began to look around her room for Kyle. She got up and made her way into the bathroom. After not finding him there or anywhere else in the hotel room, she made it back over to the bed. She sat down feeling confused as to why would he leave without letting her know. She looked over toward the nightstand and that's when she noticed the note that Kyle had left for the very first time. She reached over and after retrieving it, opened it, and began reading...

Zoe Fields,

First, I want to say that not only did I enjoy and appreciate our time spent together last night, but I enjoyed and appreciated every moment we've spent together since we've met. Last night you made me feel things that I haven't felt in years. The feelings that flooded my heart was confirmation that I've fallen in love with you. I know you're probably wondering why you've awoken without me by your side...The reason is because I've allowed my feelings of fear to override my feelings of love for the moment. The reason that I say for the moment is because as of right now I still feel as though I'm not completely ready to embark on the journey of love with anyone at this moment. I don't want to go into it with fear or reservation. I don't want to risk my indecisiveness being the cause of ruining something that has the potential of being beautiful for the long term. I know that you asked for the opportunity for us to be afraid together, but I've come to the conclusion that this fear is one that I must overcome alone in order to in the future be able to give you my love properly. I'm not sure how long it will take me to overcome this fear, but what I do know is that whenever this process is over, I'll fully be ready to embrace love with you without doubt, fear, or reservation. I understand that it would be very selfish of me to ask you to wait for me while I try figuring it out, but I know that if you do the love that I'll have to give you would be one of the most amazing loves that one could give. But if you have moved on by the time, I'm ready then I'll tell you now and again that I'm thankful for you giving me a chance to experience you. You're an amazing woman Zoe...I'll end this by saying that I love you and until next time, take care of yourself.

Love,

Kyle Malone

Zoe folded the letter back up and set it in its place. She laid her head back against the pillow and stared up at the rotating fan above. She didn't know exactly how to take the letter that Kyle had left for her. The letter caused several different emotions to hit her all at once. She picked up the letter and re-read it before placing it back on the nightstand again. Him admitting to her that he'd fallen in love with her had her mind racing. She felt that she had also fallen in love with him. She began to think about the night that they'd just shared together. After they'd made love, they laid in one another's arms and talked about everything. She had come to the conclusion in the midst of their talk that Kyle was much stronger than he cared to admit. She had firsthand knowledge on what it felt like to be confused so she knew exactly what Kyle was going through. She closed her eyes while she continued to reminisce on the night that they'd shared together. She shivered when she reminisced on his touch. He had been so soft and gentle with her. He touched, licked and kissed her perfectly. She had felt love through his touch. Throughout their night together she had determined that she would give her all to him. She felt as though she now had the opportunity to be the woman that she'd been wanting to be for a man since her late husband. After reading his letter her mind hadn't changed about giving him her all. She whispered to herself, "I'll wait for you forever if I have to," before she grabbed ahold of the pillow that he'd slept on. She brought the pillow to her nose and inhaled his scent before holding it to her chest as if it was him. Slowly, she fell back to sleep with Kyle on her mind and a smile on her face.

Cante & Louis

"What's up John? This is Louis. How are you?"

"I'm fine Louis, long time no hear from. It must be an urgent matter if I'm receiving a call from you."

"You can say that. I have someone that I really need a location on."

"Okay, what's his name?"

"Her name is Cante Light feather."

"Oh, I've never known you to have the need to locate a woman...Love calls, Huh, son?"

"I really don't want to go into details, can you find her or not?"

"I was the first person to ever find a needle in a haystack. Give me forty-five minutes max, and I'll have an exact location," finished John before ending the call. Louis stood up from his massive office chair and walked over to the window that overlooked the city. He had so many thoughts running through his mind that it was starting to give him a headache. He placed his hands behind his back, turned away from the window and began pacing the floor. He couldn't believe that he'd resorted to calling his trusty private investigator to help him locate Cante, but he felt like he had no other choice. It had been close to a month now and Cante still hadn't contacted him. His emotions were all over the place and he needed to see her and talk to her in order to get his mind back right. At first, he had begun to feel like the hell with her, but after consulting with Big Momma, he was able to put his pride to the side. Big Momma helped him to see things from both sides. She helped him understand what he would've done had he walked into Cante house and it was a strange man wrapped in only a towel. She told him to take into consideration the circumstances of their situation. How that when he'd meet her, he was a playboy and she a playgirl and that this was all new to not just him but her as well. She wanted him to understand that with both their backgrounds, trust between the two was only one missed phone call away from being gone. The sound of Louis's phone ringing broke him from his thoughts. Quickly, he answered the call. "Hello?" Hey Louis, Its John."

"Yeah, John, tell me something good."

I hope that you're ready to fuel up the jet son. The location is Northern Tijuana, Maybelline studios. A photo shoot is taking place there tomorrow at twelve noon Tijuana's time which means you need to be leaving right...about...now," finished John before hanging up. Louis instantly made another phone call to his pilot and told him to meet him at the airstrip pronto and to fuel the jet. He quickly grabbed ahold of his jacket and ran out of his office with haste.

Kyle & Zoe

Kyle sat at the end of the dock with his blue jean cutoff shorts and wife beater on, his dangling feet swinging back and forth. He held his fishing pole in his hand while looking out beyond the lake. The sky was a mixture of dark orange, dark blue and light blue as the sun settled itself in for the night. He'd been finding himself in this position a lot in the last month. He used the time to try gaining some clarity about his situation with Zoe. He felt that mentally and emotionally he couldn't focus on anything or anyone else beside her. He was at his getaway cabin in Florida. This was where he ran to when he needed a piece of mind. During this time, he took long walks on the trails, thinking mostly. Love had his mind in a twisting spiral. Zoe had come along at a time that he'd told himself that he was done with love. A time that he was completely focused and dedicated to his career solely. During his walks he questioned the timing of it all. Was it coincidence? Or was it fate that lead her to him? If it was fate, why was he fighting it so hard? He thought often about the look she had in her eyes when he stared into them, the look of fear, vulnerability and of need. The same look he knew his eyes gave off. He'd admitted to himself that he was afraid. Afraid of being twice a screwup at love. Also, he didn't want to get hurt and trusting love again opened him up to that possibility. Finally, he'd admitted to himself that he was in need of the very thing that he was running from, which was love. He reeled his fishing line in, hoping he'd gotten a bite before slinging it back out into the lake hoping for a better result. He began to wonder what Zoe thought about him and the way he left her deserted at her hotel. She probably thought that he was a jerk and he knew that he was deserving of that possibility. Deep down inside, he didn't want her feeling that way because the truth was, he longed for her love. He'd reasoned to himself that all he needed was some time alone. Some time to slow down a process that was happening way too fast for him. He stood to his feet, dropping the fishing pole on the dock. He began to walk back toward his cabin to grab another Corona. He walked inside toward the kitchen area. After opening the refrigerator, he pulled out a Corona and turned to make his way back out onto the dock. "OHHH! What the...Big Momma!!" Kyle shrieked in shock. "What the hell...I mean, what are you doing here? How'd you find me here? When did you get here?" Kyle blurted out question after question once his shock subsided.

"First off, Chilli, it's nice to see you too. Secondly, I've been here for almost two hours. I just sat at this here window and watched you on the dock. I didn't want to bother you because you looked to be deep in thought and in your own world, but since I have you here I wanted to ask you where do you keep all the pots and pans? I have to put some heat to this meal I brought along with me. I know your hungry Chilli and I brought plenty for you to eat."

"The pans are in the kitchen cupboard, to the right. They're behind the boxes. Big Momma, how'd you know where to find me?" Kyle asked questionably. "Chilli there ain't too much Big Momma don't know when it comes to you and your whereabouts. I might not always reveal myself but that doesn't mean that I don't know. Now, Chilli, could you please turn on the stove so that Big Momma could heat up these dishes and go set the table," Big Momma ordered.

Kyle began to do what he was told, and Big Momma pulled out her dishes and put them into the oven so that they could get some heat before placing them on the table. She went to wash her hands and told Kyle to do the same as they both eventually made their way to sit down and began to eat. Together, they began eating in silence. Big Momma mostly stared over the table at Kyle while he kept his eye's fixed on his plate. He knew there had to be a reason why. Big Momma had shown up to his cabin. He'd been avoiding her since his encounter with Arnold and now he'd been avoiding her because of what he'd been going through over Zoe. He began to play with his food more than eating it. Finally, he looked up and noticed Big Momma staring at him intensely.

"So, are you gonna tell Big Momma what your running from Chilli? And don't start off by saying you're not running because I know better," Finished Big Momma.

Kyle looked down at his plate again before replying. He knew that if he was gonna figure out what he needed, there was no better time than now with confiding into Big Momma. Slowly Kyle allowed his words to come out, "It's love that I'm running from Big Momma," Kyle softly replied.

"I figured as much Chilli," stated Big momma knowingly, "Love is one of the most feared and avoided emotions that humans experience. I would ask you if its Erica again, but the look in your eyes I can see that this is something different, something new, so tell me about her Chilli." Kyle looked over at Big Momma and wondered how she was. able to figure him out so easily. "Her name is Zoe and I believe that I've really fallen for her. She's so different then what I'm used to. Her approach has been different, her concern, consideration, and the things that she's been through. The look that she has in her eyes makes me want to take care of her, but what's crazy is that the look I have in my eyes seems to make her want to take care of me as well. It's all new to me and I'm afraid of it." What exactly about it are you afraid of?" "I'm afraid of the possibilities of it all." "Chilli, fear is artificial. As humans we get accustomed to allowing someone else's experiences or even our own to make us fearful. We fear because we have been taught to fear. We witness someone getting hurt riding a bike and we become fearful of that. We hear about someone drowning, so we avoid swimming. We get our heart broken and we began to fear that possibility. Chilli, are you going to allow fear to stop you from living your life?"

"I don't want to Big Momma, but what if my fear isn't artificial? What if it's just lust, that we're experiencing? It has only been a short time. What if we're both using one another to heal and once the healing is over with, we realize that we don't have anything?"

"Chilli, love doesn't have a certain time span to fully develop. I fail in love with your Poppa the first time I seen him. Love is transparent so it's not possible to mistake it for lust. Love doesn't hide itself Chilli, it lets you know when it's there and when it isn't. Love has its way of letting you know when it's the right time and when it isn't. Lust will fade away quickly, but love is relentless in its approach. When love comes for you, there's no use in hiding or running away from it. The pressure you'll feel from trying to avoid it will become unbearable, it will make you feel like you going to explode."

"That's exactly how I feel right now."

"Which is the worst feeling? The feeling you have now from running from love or the feeling you get from having it?"

"What I'm feeling now is worst. I just don't want to screw it up, I don't want to hurt her."

"If you love her Chilli then let love because pure love doesn't have ulterior motives. Pure love doesn't hurt, it doesn't betray or lie. You have to not only be real with her, but you have to be real with yourself. If you feel like you cannot be loyal to her, then don't lead her on because real love doesn't mislead. You have to first know yourself and know your intentions before you can give yourself away."
I believe I know myself and I believe, know my intentions

but I also believed the same thing before I betrayed Erica," stated Kyle.

"Chilli, you have to leave your past in the past. You cannot continue to allow it to haunt you because it will become who you are. You will not become the man that your meant to be for someone else if you can't put your old transgressions behind you. You have a love so pure inside of you, and you need to relinquish it. You need to let it flow without fear or reservation. You need to embrace it because love 'is such an amazing experience." Both Big Momma and Kyle became quite for some time as they allowed her words to sink in. After a while Big Momma asked, "Do you love her Chilli? And do you believe that she loves you?" "Yes, I do love her Big Momma and I believe that she loves me as well." "Then go get the love that you deserve and go give her the love that she deserves," finished Big Momma with authority. "Okay, Big Momma," replied Kyle with clarity.

*****

"This year has been an excellent year thanks to you two gentlemen," acknowledged Mr. Swiss to Alu and Kyle. Together they stood outside the front of Swiss Accounts awaiting their separate limousine. They'd just wrapped up their end of the period banquet and all three were full of food and champagne. "Let's repeat the same performance next year," stated Kyle.

"I second that," replied Alu.

"Yep, this is my calling," stated Mr. Swiss once he noticed his limo arriving. "Enjoy the rest of your evening fellows," ended Mr. Swiss before jumping inside the back of his limo. Once inside he loosened his tie, took a deep breath before getting comfortable. "I'm glad this day is over with," he said to himself. He reached over and grabbed a glass from one of the holders before retrieving his champagne and filling the glass. He took a gulp before staring out the window at passing streets. He sat up straight after realizing that his driver was going in the wrong direction.

"Hey, I know you're new, but you have to remember the way to my home by now and this isn't the right way," stated Mr. Swiss. He took another gulp of his champagne, "Hey," he said again once his driver didn't respond while continuing to go in the wrong direction. "Are you deaf? I said that you're going in the wrong direction!" repeated Mr. Swiss. He watched the driver pull over to the side of the rode. "What are you doing now?" asked Mr. Swiss. The driver turned in his seat suddenly.

"Wait a minute, you're not my driver."

Before Mr. Swiss realized what was happening, he got struck in the head with a blunt object that the driver was holding, knocking him unconscious instantly.

When Mr. Swiss came to, he blinked continuously while trying to clear his blurry vision. He tried to stand to his feet but felt restrained. Next, he tried to touch the place on his head that the blood seemed to be coming from but again he felt restrained. "what the hell is going on here?" he said aloud. He looked down at the straps that tied his hands and feet together. The wooden chair that he was strapped to rocked back and forth as he tried freeing himself. "Dad," said a voice off in the distance. "Dad, I'm glad to have you here, I've really missed you."

"Who's there?" asked Mr. Swiss. "I'm no one's father," he relayed.

The man walked from behind Mr. Swiss clear into his vision.

"Dad, I've missed you," the man said.

"Mr. Simmons? What's going on here? Why do you have me bound?"

"My names Mr. Simmons Jr., Mr. Simmons Sr. was killed."

"Okay, but what does any of this have to do with me? And why have you kidnapped me?"

"It's been a long-time dad, I've missed you. I was lost without you, but I've found my way dad...I've found the way."

"What are you talking about Mr. Simmons? I'm not your father, your delusional." Arnold walked within inches of a bound Mr. Swiss before he began to speak. "I was twelve years old the morning that I walked up to my father's study, I heard him in the midst of a heated argument about the acquisition of what has now been renamed Swiss pharmaceuticals..." Arnold paused and allowed his words to sink in to Mr. Swiss. The revelation showed clearly on Mr. Swiss's face.

"Little Arnold?!? Oh my god..."stated Mr. Swiss in shock.

"Yes, Little Arnold, the son of Arnold Lamount Simmons Sr. which is the very man that you killed because of greed..." stated Arnold furiously.

"That wasn't the way things were supposed to go, trust me."

"Well tell me exactly how it was supposed to go," demanded Arnold.

"We just wanted to scare him, but your father wouldn't give in to the pressure. We tried everything before it got to that point. He wouldn't accept our bribe to back out of the bidding war. We had no choice, it was either get rid of him or lose out on and investment that had gross potential of billions," replied Mr. Swiss.

"So instead of losing out on an investment, you decide to take my father's life," asked Arnold angrily.

"I'm sorry son, I'm so sorry. I've regretted that decision for years and I'm haunted everyday by the blood that is on my hands." "Don't call me son, you son of a bitch. You killed my father; don't you dare call me son," shouted Arnold right before he pulled out his gun and pointed it at Mr. Swiss's head...

To be continued.......

Epilogue: Love Have Mercy On Me Too…..

[Arnold sat disoriented on the hard wood flooring while sweating profusely. He couldn't hear or see anything around him, and he felt as if he were having an otter body experience. The only sense he had was of feeling. The feeling of his heart beating wildly, the feeling of sweat dripping from his face and finally, the feeling of the rubber grip pistol that he was holding. Quickly he released the gun from his grip like it was infected. Did he really? Had he really just taken a life? That couldn't be possible he thought to himself. Frantically he began looking around, he looked for signs of familiarity but found none. Next, he tried making it to his feet, but the weakness that he felt inside himself wouldn't permit it. "Dad!" he managed to scream out. "Dad, where are you?" Hysterically he began looking around for his father, where was he? "Dad!" he yelled out again before looking down at his hands. He noticed that his hands were covered in blood. The sight of all the blood made him panic even more. He didn't know where he was, he didn't know where his father was, all he did know was that he did something terribly wrong. Had he blacked out? Had he, had he killed someone? "It couldn't be," he said to himself while trying to make it to his feet. He gathered himself and as he stood, he staggered slightly. He began wobbling around the mostly empty room, trying to find a sense of life. A sharp pain shot through his head and it brought him back down to his knees. He brought his hands up to his head to try stopping the pain...Mr. Swiss. The image of Mr. Swiss struck him. Was it...Was it Mr. Swiss that he'd killed? He'd remembered seeing him, but where was he now? Was this all of his blood? Once the pain subsided in Arnold's head, he made it back to his feet. Stumbling, he made it to a doorway off to the side of the room. He looked in and seen blood all over the floor. He broke down to his knees again and was hit with the same head pain from earlier but worst this time. He tried opening his eyes, but he couldn't. "Dad!" he managed to scream out again before forcing his eyes open. This time there was no mistaking what he'd seen. The body at the end of that trail of blood was lifeless. He began crawling on all fours, trying to make it to the deceased. With each crawl the pain in his head intensified. He began to yell, he yelled out for the pain to stop, he yelled out begging for strength to get him over to the life that he'd taken. Finally, he doubled over. He began to cry. He cried long and hard sobs that echoed throughout the warehouse. He cried out in regret, in pain and in sorrow. He didn't intend to harm anyone. He wasn't violent by nature but had found himself in a position as to where violence was necessary. Slowly, he turned himself around facing the lifeless body once again, the sight made him vomit involuntarily. He began to think of his father and how someone once took his life. He'd always told himself that he wouldn't become the same type of animal as the person that killed his father. But now, he was. He reached inside his pocket in search of his phone. Once he located it, he dialed nine one one before putting it to his ear.

"Nine one one dispatch, what is your emergency?" asked the dispatcher. "I've just killed someone," replied Arnold.

"Can you please give me your location and tell me who is it that you've killed?"

"I... I... I don't know my location and I can't see who it is exactly that I've killed, but I know I killed them, responded Arnold disoriented.

"What is your name sir?"

"Arnold Lamount Simmons Jr," responded Arnold before ending the call.]

Also Available by Bagz of Money Content

Live by It, Die by It (By: Ice Money)

Mercenary (By: Ice Money)

The Ruler of the Red Ruler (By: Kutta)

Block Boyz (By: Juvi)

Team Savage (By Ace Boogie)

Team Savage 2 (By Ace Boogie)

Rich Pride (By M.L. Moore)

Available at Bagzofmoneycontent.com and most major bookstores.